Anonymous

Queen of the Lakes

Buffalo, the Electric City of the Future

Anonymous

Queen of the Lakes
Buffalo, the Electric City of the Future

ISBN/EAN: 9783337324865

Printed in Europe, USA, Canada, Australia, Japan

Cover: Foto ©Andreas Hilbeck / pixelio.de

More available books at **www.hansebooks.com**

QUEEN OF THE LAKES ...

BUFFALO

THE ELECTRIC CITY
OF THE FUTURE ...

SOUVENIR

OF THE TENTH CONVEN-
TION OF THE NATIONAL
ASSOCIATION OF BUILDERS

SEPTEMBER 14, 15, 16, 17, 18 and 19
···· 1896 ····

THE COURIER COMPANY,
DESIGNERS,
ENGRAVERS,
PRINTERS,
BUFFALO, NEW YORK.

WELCOME TO BUFFALO.

PROGRAMME ....

FOR ENTERTAINMENT OF GUESTS AND VISITORS TO THE TENTH ANNUAL CONVENTION. ... ...

The General Committee, appointed by the Builders' Association Exchange with full power to devise a plan of entertainment that would not conflict with the work of the Tenth Annual Convention of the National Association of Builders, but furnish to the delegates and visitors such entertainment as would show the many advantages of this growing city, and the immense electric power that in a short time will be placed within its limits, desire that, in carrying out the programme, more or less of a social feature should be included, so that when our guests shall have returned to their homes, it cannot be said of us that "all work and no play makes Jack a dull boy."

PROGRAMME

OF

ENTERTAINMENT IN DETAIL.

Monday, September 14th, 1896.
OPEN HOUSE— . . . . Rooms Builders' Exchange.

Tuesday, September 15th.
THEATRE PARTY— . . . . Evening, Star Theatre.

Wednesday, September 16th.
CARRIAGE RIDE—Leaving Hotel Iroquois at 2.30 P. M. *sharp.*

Thursday, September 17th.
TRIP TO NIAGARA FALLS—Boat leaving foot of Main Street at 9 A. M. *sharp,* for an all-day trip.

Friday, September 18th.
LADIES' BANQUET— . . . Hotel Iroquois, at 9 P. M.

GENTLEMEN'S RECEPTION AND SMOKER—German-American Hall, at 8.30 P. M.

Headquarters.

Opening Monday, Sept. 14th. and for the entire week.

LADIES— . . . Ladies' Parlor, Hotel Iroquois.

GENTLEMEN—Rooms Nos. 11, 12, 13 and 14, Builders' Exchange.

NATIONAL ASSOCIATION PROGRAMME.

See last pages of Book.

GENERAL COMMITTEE

OF THE

BUILDERS' ASSOCIATION EXCHANGE

IN CHARGE OF ENTERTAINMENT

OF THE NATIONAL ASSOCIATION OF BUILDERS, AT
THE TENTH CONVENTION.

CHARLES A. RUPP, . . *Chairman.*
GEO. W. CARTER, . *Treasurer.*
J. C. ALMENDINGER, . . *Secretary.*

ALFRED LYTH,   JOHN FEIST,
GEO. DUCHSCHERER,   H. C. HARROWER,
A. A. BERRICK,   H. RUMRILL, JR.
CHARLES GEIGER,   F. P. JONES.

Special Committees.

HALL.

ALFRED LYTH, *Chairman,*
WILLIAM H. BRUSH,   GEO. ENGEL.

SOUVENIRS AND PRINTING.

H. C. HARROWER, *Chairman,*
F. T. COPPINS,   GEO. H. DUNBAR.

HOTELS.

GEO. DUCHSCHERER, *Chairman,*
HENRY E. BOLLER,   W. S. GRATTAN,

EXCURSIONS.

H. Rumrill, Jr., *Chairman,*

Geo. C. Fox,   Alvin W. Day.

THEATRES.

A. A. Berrick, *Chairman,*

Frank W. Carter,   J. C. Almendinger.

BICYCLES.

F. P. Jones, *Chairman,*

C. B. Jameson,   M. Scheeler.

CARRIAGES.

Charles Geiger, *Chairman,*

Peter Ginther,   Henry Wendt.

RECEPTION AND SMOKER.

John Feist, *Chairman,*

John W. Henrich,   W. H. Kurtz.

ENTERTAINMENT OF LADIES.

Geo. W. Carter, *Chairman,*

J. H. Tilden,   Charles W. Adams,

Geo. W. Maltby,   C. C. Calkins,

H. E. Montgomery.

COMMITTEES

FOR

SPECIAL ENTERTAINMENT OF VARIOUS DELEGATIONS.

COLORS FOR GUESTS AND FOR MEMBERS OF COMMITTEES WILL CORRESPOND.

Committee to Entertain Delegates from Baltimore.

Colors for Baltimore—LIGHT BLUE.

JACOB REIMANN, *Chairman*,

A. MACHWIRTH,	J. W. DANFORTH,
GEO. KEMPF,	A. J. HOFFMEYER,
D. PAUL HUGHES,	OTTO CARL,
WALTER CARY,	S. L. GRAVES.

Committee to Entertain Delegates from Boston.

Colors for Boston—VIOLET.

J. J. CHURCHYARD, *Chairman*,

P. P. BURTIS,	E. L. COOK,
J. W. DWYER,	AVERY C. WOLFE,
FRANK L. BEYER,	JOHN LORENZ, JR.
MAURICE E. PREISCH,	G. ELIAS,
CHARLES B. HUCK,	GEO. B. MONTGOMERY,
JOHN H. BLACK,	JOHN C. BERTRAND,
NELSON C. SPENCER,	EDWARD VOISARD.

Committee to Entertain Delegates from Chicago.

Colors for Chicago—DARK BLUE.

WM. D. COLLINGWOOD, *Chairman,*

LAWRENCE GINTHER,	HENRY L. JONES,
A. P. KEHR,	CHRISTIAN BRENNER,
FRED. A. MENGE,	VALENTINE METZ,
CHARLES MOSIER,	WM. M. SAVAGE,
WM. E. CARROLL,	LOUIS A. FISCHER,
PETER H. FRANK,	A. G. NORTHEN.

Committee to Entertain Delegates from Detroit.

Colors for Detroit—PINK.

GEO. M. STOWE, *Chairman,*

GEO. H. PETERS, JR.,	ALFRED J. SPARKES,
CHARLES A. RCHARDSON,	JOHN C. WATSON,
EDWARD H. ROOS,	J. L. LANE,
CHARLES A. SMITH,	WM. F. BRAY,
JOHN L. BANNISTER,	JOS. F. HOFFMEYER.

Committee to Entertain Delegates from Lowell.

Colors for Lowell—PURPLE.

GEO. E. FRANK, *Chairman,*

JOSEPH KLAUS,	E. MARCHESINI,
WM. M. LUTHER,	M. N. SMITH,

WM. H. LYTH.

Committee to Entertain Delegates from Milwaukee.

Colors for Milwaukee—YELLOW.

JOHN LANNEN, *Chairman*,

ALFRED W. THORN,	GEO. W. SCHMIDT,
J. H. ROSS,	M. A. REEB,
JAMES S. COCKBURN,	C. P. BARNWELL,
FRED. HENRICH,	HENRY HUMMELL.

Committee to Entertain Delegates from New York.

Colors for New York—ORANGE.

HENRY SCHAEFER, *Chairman*,

JOHN F. BERRICK,	JOSEPH F. STABELL,
M. McNAMARA,	DANIEL McGINNIS,
JOHN S. NOYES,	WILLIAM H. CARTER,
JOSEPH C. HENAFELT,	C. M. HELMER,
ANGUS McLEAN,	THOMAS BROWN,

JAMES N. BYERS.

Committee to Entertain Delegates from Philadelphia.

Colors for Philadelphia—SILVER GRAY.

EDWARD M. HAGER, *Chairman*,

J. N. SCATCHERD,	HARVEY J. HURD,
M. BERGMAN,	CARL MEYER,
FRANK L. GEORGER,	HENRY SMITH,
GEO. IRLBACKER,	EMIL MACHWIRTH,
HARRY C. PARSONS,	O. B. McNAMARA,
S. E. PLEWES,	J. M. WILSON,
L. C. LITCHFIELD,	O. S. LAYCOCK.

Committee to Entertain Delegates from Providence.

Colors for Providence--BROWN.

B. I. CROOKER, *Chairman,*

A. B. PENFIELD,	F. H. GROVE,
WM. H. PINCK,	C. T. DENNIS,
ROBERT F. SHERMAN,	WM. STOKES,
JACOB HASSELBECK,	EDWARD R. FLACH.

Committee to Entertain Delegates from Rochester.

Colors for Rochester—OLIVE.

N. C. BARNUM, *Chairman,*

E. H. GARDNER,	GEORGE KELLER,
CHAS. F. ERNST,	JOHN LOEWER,
D. R. FOGELSONGER,	WM. H. FITZPATRICK,
J. G. HELBLING,	HARRY S. WELSH,
JACOB JAECKLE,	JAMES S. BOWES,
LOUIS H. DAVIS,	WM. SCHUMACHER,

E. P. SMITH.

Committee to Entertain Delegates from St. Louis.

Colors for St. Louis--LAVENDER.

M. J. BYRNE, *Chairman,*

L. P. BEYER,	CHAS. M. GALLE,
D. J. DONAVAN,	JACOB L. MENSCH,
WM. N. SMITH,	JOHN RITTER,
GEO. B. BATES,	A. O'NEILL.

Committee to Entertain Delegates from St. Paul.

Colors for St. Paul—TERRA COTTA.

JAMES S. STYGALL, JR., *Chairman*,

G. M. BOOTH,
GEO. NACHTRIEB,

CHARLES E. FERGUSON,
H. DIETSCHLER, JR.

Committee to Entertain Delegates from Wilmington.

Colors for Wilmington—SCARLET.

R. E. BURGER, *Chairman*,

G. W. FOLGER,
JOHN GESL, JR.,

J. E. ROONEY,
GEO. M. MISNER,

A. J. BATT.

Committee to Entertain Delegates from Worcester.

Colors for Worcester—DARK GREEN.

LESLIE BENNETT, *Chairman*,

WILLIAM H. SCHMIDT,
FRED. LUEDEMAN,
GEO. J. HAGER,
PAUL SCHUEFFNER,
F. M. HILL,

ANTHONY BATT,
T. H. FLACH,
N. NIEDERPRUEM,
GEO. W. VOSS,
BENJAMIN REIMANN.

Committee to Entertain Visitors from Associations not Affiliated with the National Association.

Colors for Visitors—WHITE.

The President of the National Association,
CHARLES A. RUPP,

The President of the Builders' Association Exchange,
ALFRED LYTH,

The Secretary of the Builders' Association Exchange,
J. C. ALMENDINGER,

CHRISTIAN W. SCHAEFER,	J. L. KRONENBERG,
E. C. RUMRILL,	FRED. BARND,
GEO. FLYNN,	C. W. HOLLOWAY,
LYMAN COPPINS,	P. SCHEELER.

Committee of Ladies to Entertain Visiting Ladies.

Colors for Ladies—RED, WHITE AND BLUE.

MRS. CHARLES A. RUPP, *Chairman,*
MISS CHARLOTTE S. TILDEN, *Secretary,*

MRS. GEO. W. CARTER,	MRS. JOHN FEIST,
MRS. HENRY E. BOLLER,	MRS, ALFRED LYTH,
MRS. H. E. MONTGOMERY,	MRS. ANNA GEHRES,
MRS. HENRY SCHAEFER,	MRS. GEO. W. MALTBY,
MRS. ALFRED A. BERRICK,	MRS. F. T. COPPINS,
MRS. ROBERT E. BURGER,	MRS. JACOB REIMANN,
MRS. JOHN LANNEN,	MRS. GEORGE FLYNN,
MRS. C. C. CALKINS,	MISS LUCY REIMANN.

Committee to Entertain the National Association of Builders and Inspectors of Buildings.

Colors—PINK, ON LIGHT BLUE.

JOHN CARTER, *Chairman*,

JOHN IRLBACKER,	HENRY REULING,
WM. LAUTZ,	JOHN LORENZ, SR.,
JOHN O'CONNOR,	WM. F. WENDT,
A. C. KRANICHFELD,	CHAS. K. FOSTER,

E. C. LUFKIN.

NOTES.

The General Committee will have general supervision of all interests, and wear the local button with white ribbon, with the words "General Committee."

The Special Committees will wear the local button with white ribbon, with the words "Special Committee."

The several committees in charge of visiting delegations will wear the local button of the Buffalo Exchange, together with the color or colors which distinguish the delegations they are assigned to.

All delegates and visitors will wear the National Association button, with the color or colors assigned to their delegation.

By this means the respective Buffalo committees will be enabled to distinguish the guests they have in charge, and *vice versa*.

The committee of ladies will wear the Buffalo button, with a knot of red, white and blue ribbon, and will furnish the National button with the same colors to each of the visiting ladies.

The gentlemen assigned to assist the committee of ladies will wear the Buffalo button, with the red, white and blue colors.

The chairmen of the several committees will, immediately upon the arrival of their delegations, secure a list of the names of the ladies and gentlemen comprising the party, delivering this list to the Secretary, who will issue the Souvenir Books and distinguishing badges upon receipt of same.

Index of Colors of Distinguishing Badges.

LIGHT BLUE,	BALTIMORE.
VIOLET,	BOSTON.
DARK BLUE,	CHICAGO.
PINK,	DETROIT.
PURPLE,	LOWELL.
YELLOW,	MILWAUKEE.
ORANGE,	NEW YORK.
SILVER GRAY,	PHILADELPHIA.
BROWN,	PROVIDENCE.
OLIVE,	ROCHESTER.
LAVENDER,	ST. LOUIS.
TERRA COTTA,	ST. PAUL.
SCARLET,	WILMINGTON.
DARK GREEN,	WORCESTER.
RED, WHITE AND BLUE,	LADIES.

WHITE, MISCELLANEOUS ASSOCIATIONS AND VISITORS NOT AFFILIATED WITH THE NATIONAL ASSOCIATION.

PINK ON LIGHT BLUE, NATIONAL ASSOCIATION OF COMMISSIONERS AND INSPECTORS OF BUILDINGS.

WHITE, WITH WORDS "GENERAL COMMITTEE, BUFFALO."

WHITE, WITH WORDS "SPECIAL COMMITTEE, BUFFALO."

ENTRANCE TO BUFFALO HARBOR.

BUFFALO.

Its Early History.

AFTER his visit to this country in the year 1804, Tom
Moore wrote a weird "Song of the Evil Spirit of the
Woods," telling of sprites, agues and wolves, with which
he coupled this note: "The idea of this poem occurred
to me in passing through the very dreary wilderness
between Batavia—a new settlement in the midst of the
woods—and the little village of Buffalo, on Lake Erie.
This is the most fatiguing part of the journey through
the Genesee country to Niagara." The statement must
seem almost incredible to one who traverses the territory referred to now. True, by turning from the direct
line, a fragment of the Tonawanda swamp may be found,
but mainly, in the place of the wilderness, there is a land
as smiling, as really flowing with milk and honey, as that
which Moses saw from the mountain. Desolation has
given way to life's keenest activities.

In a later year, regarding the same expedition, the poet
wrote further: "The latter part of the journey, which
lay chiefly through yet but half-cleared woods, we were
obliged to perform on foot, and a slight accident I met
with, in the course of our rugged walk, laid me up for
some days at Buffalo. To the rapid growth in that won-
derful region, of, at least, the materials of civilization—
however ultimately they may be turned to account—this
flourishing town, which stands on Lake Erie, bears most
ample testimony. Though little better, at the time when I

visited it, than a mere village, consisting chiefly of huts and wigwams, it is now, by all accounts, a populous and splendid city, with five or six churches, town hall, theatre, and other such appurtenances of a capital."

These quotations add to other evidence that from its earliest days the settlement at Buffalo Creek was the better known, both at home and abroad, as Buffalo, notwithstanding the attempt of its founder to fasten a Dutch city's name upon it.

When the wandering bard visited the Niagara frontier, it was well upon the outposts of American civilization, and a weary journey from tidewater, or even the central New York settlements; still there were villages here and in Canada, at the mouth of the Niagara river, and some business, as well as houses of entertainment, in the neighborhood of the Falls. But Buffalo had only begun to make history. Previous to the Revolutionary War, no white man permanently dwelt here, and, indeed, there is little more than legend regarding the Indian occupants of the vicinity until the coming of the Senecas to settle on Buffalo Creek, after Sullivan, with fire and sword, had wasted the fertile district of their former abode.

Explorers had visited the place of the present city; armed forces had encamped upon it, and as early as 1763 an engagement took place here between Indians and British soldiers. When the Senecas came, they brought several white captives, who made their home in the Indian village, and tilled the soil for their red masters. Within a hundred years, what changes, what development! Of the dead past of the preceding century, how few, disconnected, and incomplete the records! Misty traditions; a few arrow-heads. On the 17th of August, 1679, the

VIEW OF BUFFALO RIVER AND ELEVATORS.

chivalric French warrior and explorer. La Salle, entered Lake Erie on the "Griffon," which, with infinite labor, his few followers had built and launched from the east side of Niagara River, at Cayuga Creek, about three miles south of the Falls. The craft was of sixty tons burthen, and bore thirty-four men and seven cannon, which had been brought from Fort Niagara. So this ship of the wilderness spread its sails, a hundred and thirty-nine years before the first crude steamboat of the lakes proved the fitness of her name of "Walk-in-the-Water."

The first full-blooded white settler of Buffalo was Cornelius Winney, an Albany trader, who established himself in a log-cabin store in 1792. In 1796, there are said to have been three white residents.

New Amsterdam.

The purchase from Massachusetts of title to lands in Western New York by Phelps and Gorham, and their subsequent embarrassment, led to a brief ownership of the site by Robert Morris, the financier of the Revolution. In 1792-3 it passed from him to the so-called Holland Land Company, a group of Dutch capitalists, who had lent money to the Continental government. An agency was opened at Batavia. Joseph Ellicott was the first agent, and he was Buffalo's founder. He gave to the cluster of huts at the mouth of Buffalo Creek the name of New Amsterdam, bestirring himself to attract immigration to it.

Ellicott was a man of exceeding foresight, as well as energy. In New Amsterdam he saw the seed of a great city. Few are the prophets whose forecasts have been realized so completely. In 1803 he surveyed and laid out the town, planning a system of streets which might have been adhered to with more wisdom than has been shown by some of his successors in authority. Also he devised numerous schemes for the improvement and embellishment of the place. They were not consummated, because, perhaps, they were ahead of their time. He was an enthusiast in his conviction of the future importance of the new city at the foot of Lake Erie, but misfortune and a sorrowful end were his long before the fullness of his dream became true. "God has made Buffalo, and I must try to make Batavia," Ellicott is reported to have said. Again, he was asked whether he thought Batavia would always surpass Buffalo. "That is to ask," he replied, "whether the local office of the Holland Company or the power of Almighty God is the greater."

The geography was right for his conviction, but prophetic vision was needed to see the great march of civilization to the setting sun, that must open up the vast territory of the real West before there would be argosies' on Lake Erie's bosom. The lake and river were here, still there was practically no harbor, for Buffalo Creek entered Lake Erie through marsh lands, and its mouth was closed by a sand-bar, which sometimes a skiff could hardly cross. This situation was not improved until twenty years after Ellicott's survey of 1803. The village was called New Amsterdam in honor of the Dutch holders of the Holland Purchase. Streets were named for individual countrymen of Father Knickerbocker, but staid and ever-smoking Dutch burghers did not people them. New Amsterdam was Dutch only by courtesy. The settlers came from New England and the New York State peopled parts.

A COAL TRESTLE.

where increasing numbers inspired the movement forward. The name of New Amsterdam did not fit; nor did the names of Schimmelpennick and Vollenhoven avenues and Stadnitzki street. Buffalo Creek had been known as such from earliest tradition. Buffalo was the logical name for the town. As to its origin, there has been much of speculation and controversy; and as to whether the haplessly almost extinct American bison did ever herd in this locality, local savants of good repute have proved the affirmative—at least to their own satisfaction.

Buffalo Village.

By act of March 11th, 1808, New Amsterdam became Buffalo, and the county seat of Niagara County, which was then created. This enactment was conditional that the Holland Company should deed the county not less than half an acre of land for public buildings, and should erect thereon a court-house and jail. The company complied, constructing a court-house of wood and a jail of stone. The former building was burned by the British in 1813. After the war, a new one was erected on Washington street—the "Old Court-house"—which in its long history was the place of momentous scenes and knew many eminent people.

The next few years of the village tell only the old, uninteresting story of the struggles and vicissitudes of pioneers in a time of peace. With their Indian neighbors they never had serious trouble. Indeed, the relations between the Senecas and the people of Buffalo were, on almost all occasions, of the friendliest. The great chiefs, Cornplanter, Farmer's Brother, the famous orator Red Jacket,

and others of distinction, were familiar to the village
streets in the long ago. In this later generation, their
bones have been gathered into a spot in beautiful Forest
Lawn, which a stately monument with bronze statue of
Red Jacket marks. To this day there are descendants in
considerable number of the Six Nations, on the Catta-
raugus and Tonawanda Reservations, not far from Buffalo;
but the deterioration of the race in Western New York is
apparent, in the fact that in the last half century but one
of these Indians has risen to importance.

Burned by the British.

War came between the United States and Great Britain.
It brought to the people of Buffalo a season of much
misery, with little either of honor or success to lighten
this page of the village record. The events of 1813-14
on this frontier are in the national history, and, save the
local catastrophe, need not be dwelt upon here.

In 1813-14, some of the hardest fighting of the war
occurred on the Niagara frontier, notably at Queenston, at
Lundy's Lane, at Chippewa and at Fort Erie. At the
mouth of the river, opposite Buffalo, are the picturesque
remains of the old fortification, the possession of which
was the motive of several sanguinary struggles. The
star-shaped earthworks are still clearly defined, and frag-
ments of the walls of the stone block-house, within the
embankment, yet stand. In all the enumerated important
engagements, the United States soldiers acquitted themselves with gallantry and good measure of success. But
little Buffalo's inhabitants suffered inglorious disaster,
before competent officers were at the front to effectively
direct the military operations.

THE OLD FILLMORE RESIDENCE.

A first attack on Buffalo was repulsed. But a little later, on the 30th of December, 1813, a British force of eight hundred regulars and two hundred Canadian Indians, under Major-General Riall, crossed the Niagara and advanced upon the village. The American regulars had been withdrawn to Batavia. There remained a force of some two thousand undisciplined militia, inadequately supplied with ammunition, of whom eight hundred deserted as soon as hostilities became imminent. But a feeble attempt at defense was made. The villagers loaded such household effects as they could into wagons and fled. Scarcely had they departed before the hostile Indians began their work of pillage and incendiarism. The town was ordered burned in retaliation for the recent destruction of Newark (now Niagara, Ont.) by Col. McClure. On every road leading to safety, " were little processions of terrified villagers, fleeing from the savage foe into the embrace of the wintry forest. Who shall tell what they suffered—these houseless fugitives, ignorant of the fate of father, husband, brother, by day skulking through the forest, and at night creeping under the roof of some friendly Indian hut." Thirty men were reported as killed by the invaders, forty wounded, and sixty-nine made prisoners.

Arisen from Her Ashes.

On April 5th, the *Gazette*—first newspaper of the Niagara frontier—which had been removed to Williamsville, made this announcement: " Buffalo village which once adorned the shores of Erie, and was prostrated by the enemy, is now rising again."

Gradually the people returned and rebuilt their homes. Another attempt was made to capture Buffalo, but failed.

On the 16th of September, the sortie was made by the garrison of Fort Erie, by which the British forces investing it were routed, and their batteries captured, the enemy's loss being six hundred killed and wounded. "It was a fierce contest, in which the elements fought even more fiercely than the blood-thirsty mortals, and was by far the most brilliant encounter on the Niagara frontier during the war. The tidings of the great victory brought joy to the surviving Buffalonians, and four days later the British raised the siege hereabouts and retired to Fort George. The war was practically over, so far as Buffalo's vital interests were concerned."

In July, 1815, the *Gazette* reported that as many houses had been erected in Buffalo, or were in course of erection, as were burned a year and a half before. Building was also begun with vigor by Buffalo's quondam rival, Black Rock. The year 1816 brought the memorable "cold summer." It caused the failure of all crops in the neighborhood, and Buffalo felt its effects seriously. "The trade that had fallen off largely with the departure of the army, was now still further reduced, and an era of hard times began that effectually retarded the growth of the village for a period of five years. While money was plenty many had become involved in debt, which they now found themselves unable to pay. Flour sold in Buffalo at fifteen dollars a barrel, and other provisions were comparatively high in price." The *Gazette* of August 20th, stated that there was "not a barrel of breadstuff in the village for sale." In the words of a resident at the time, " a scene of

VIEW AT THE FRONT.

insolvency ensued. more distressing, if possible, than even the destruction of the village."

But a project was being revived which was destined to put new life into the stagnant hamlet ; the construction of a canal across the State from Lake Erie to the Hudson river, with its western terminus at either Buffalo or Black Rock. The first survey was made from Buffalo to the Genesee, in the summer of 1816, and the work thereafter was pushed with vigor. Not until 1820, however, were Buffalo and Black Rock measurably affected by the prospect of the canal's early completion.

The "Walk-in-the-Water."

The pioneer lake steamer, the "Walk-in-the-Water," was launched at Black Rock, on May 28th, 1818, and was ready for business about the middle of August. Besides her engine, she was fitted with two masts and sails. Steam power, as developed in this primitive craft, was not strong enough to contend with the Niagara's current, and she had to be towed up to the lake. From the first, the boat was successful financially. The fare to Detroit was fixed at eighteen dollars for cabin and seven dollars for steerage passengers. She took out one hundred and twenty passengers on her second trip. On the 1st of November, 1821, the "Walk-in-the-Water" was wrecked off the Buffalo lighthouse.

First Harbor Improvement.

Buffalo had a formidable rival in Black Rock—long since swallowed by the city whose bounds are far beyond the one-time competitor's old lines. Black Rock had a natural harbor—such as it was and is. Buffalo's harbor needed costly development to become serviceable. Steamboats landed and took on passengers at Black Rock ; vessels discharged their cargoes there, then were towed up against the strong current, to the lake, by teams of oxen. Buffalo's best citizens realized the situation. They sought an appropriation from the State for the improvement of the harbor, but it was refused ; so they took the work into their own hands, literally. Professional men, business men, laborers, turned out with shovels and axes, and actually constructed a pier of fascines, to keep the sand away from the mouth of the creek. Others contributed money, or goods to be converted into money, for the undertaking. A gale came and turned the pier upside down in the very gaze of its makers ; but it was securely anchored to its position, and in the spring of 1822 the steamer "Superior," which was built on the creek's bank with the strict guaranty that she should not be detained by lack of water, was enabled to pass out upon the lake. Such was the beginning of Buffalo's harbor improvement, upon which millions have been expended and which is not yet completed. The opening of the creek to the passage of vessels, and the designation of Buffalo instead of Black Rock as the western terminus of the canal, settled the question of supremacy for all time.

Buffalo village was incorporated April 2, 1813; was re-organized in 1815, and again in 1822. In 1825 it had 2,412 inhabitants.

" The Three Thayers."

That year, 1825, was a notable one in Buffalo's early history. On June 17th, the three Thayers were marched, to music of fife and drum, from the old jail down Court

THE PARK LAKE.

street to a common of which Niagara Square was a part, and were there hanged in the presence of a great throng of spectators. The culprits were of a low class of farmers; their victim was an obscure peddler, one John Love; the crime was brutal, and for the most sordid motive; but the extraordinary event of the execution of three brothers, on one gallows, created a great sensation. From all directions people came long distances, in all sorts of vehicles, to witness the gruesome free show. For two-thirds of a century afterwards, the hanging of the three Thayers was to old folks a chronological guide-board that often aided failing memory.

The Erie Canal.

Another event of 1825, and of immeasurably higher importance, was the completion of the Erie Canal—the Grand Canal, as it was then called—on the 24th of October. This great water-way, which more than anything else has enabled New York to maintain her position as the Empire State, did not at once affect Buffalo as beneficially as had been expected. Little freight was carried for some time, the business being chiefly in the transportation of passengers; but with the lapse of a few years the value of the water-way to Buffalo as well as to the State and Nation was fully demonstrated. Its usefulness was substantially increased by the enlargement in 1836.

Morgan's Disappearance.

The " Morgan Excitement " was the sensation of 1826-27. William Morgan of Batavia, having announced the intention of exposing in a book the secrets of the order, was abducted by Free Masons, taken to Fort Niagara, which was then unoccupied, and, it is generally believed, put to death by drowning in the Niagara River. The excitement attained such heat that the anti-Masonry issue entered into the State politics, and as an anti-Mason, Millard Fillmore, afterwards President of the United States, first entered public life as a legislator.

Buffalo a City.

On the 20th of April, 1832, Buffalo, having attained a population of over 10,000, was incorporated as a city, with Ebenezer Johnson as the first Mayor. Its municipal career began in a time of trouble and dread, for that year brought a direful visitation of cholera, which carried may estimable citizens to their graves. The disease was disastrously epidemic again in 1834, one of the victims being Buffalo's second Mayor, Major A. Andrews. One morning he, his wife and their daughter, were discovered dead in their home, which stood to the east of Main street, in the vicinity of Huron street. While there were some heroic women and men who went forth to attend the sick and lay out the dead, the great number of the inhabitants were terror-stricken, and the miseries of the period were long remembered. But the canal business was now flourishing ; a large fleet of steamers plied upon the lake, and Buffalo went right on growing. In 1835 the population was nearly 20,000, having more than doubled in five years.

" The next year," says a local historian, " the inevitable real estate speculation, which had begun in 1833, reached its height. It was an era of wild inflation all over the country, and in many cities prices were realized for land

BRIDGE VIEW—THE PARK.

which have never since been paralleled. The local excitement was intensified by the discovery of large forgeries by
the chief of the speculators, Benjamin Rathbun, proprietor
of the Eagle Tavern." Rathbun, like many others, meant
to repay, but was unable to do so before the exposure
came. He was a man of much ability, and really did a
great deal for the city. After serving his sentence of five
years in the State prison, he went to New York city, where
he was long the keeper of Rathbun's Hotel, on Broadway,
and quite re-instated himself in the public's respect.

The panic of 1837, which the fever of speculation
brought on the nation, divided local attention with the
Canadian rebellion, known as the "Patriots' War," owing
to the occupation of Navy Island, in the Niagara River,
by the Patriots, and the destruction by their enemies of the
steamer "Caroline," while on the American side of the
stream. The resulting excitement caused the formation
of one of Buffalo's military organizations, and brought to
the scene Gen. Winfield Scott, with a brilliant staff. There
was no fighting on this side of the line, and five military
weddings were the chief local outcome of the Patriots'
War.

First Railroad—First Elevator.

In 1842 came the first railroad, the Buffalo & Attica. It
was thirty miles long. The line is now incorporated in the
Erie system. The Erie, some years later, made Dunkirk
its western terminus, because Buffalo would not accede to
all its demands ; but the corporation could not successfully combat nature and make Dunkirk instead of Buffalo
the great place of transfer of the products of the West.
In due time the Erie saw fit to construct a line to this city,

in order to get a share of the traffic. At a still later time, the New York Central sought to coerce the municipality, and more effectively, by removing its passenger station to a point three miles away from the business center. The passenger terminus was changed back again to Exchange street after the company had obtained the gift of an invaluable franchise across the lower part of the city.

In that year the first grain elevator was begun by Joseph Dart, who applied an old principle to a new use, with results of almost incomprehensible importance. A cargo of grain from a lake vessel at that time was at the most only five thousand or six thousand bushels ; but to transfer it with sacks and shovels as the only appliances was a task that required much time. To-day, one of the big elevators, operated practically the same as Dart operated his little one, will empty a great steamship of more than a hundred thousand bushels of wheat in a few hours. This done, the ship may receive two thousand or more tons of coal at one of the vast trestles, for an up freight, and be ready to clear the same night.

Buffalo continued to grow, although not with the rapidity that some had expected, and thrived well until the completion of trunk line railroads from the seaboard to the West. The lake and canal passenger business contributed immensely to her activity. The freight business had not grown to be of more than secondary note. Great and splendid side-wheel steamers were built, such as the "Western World" and "Plymouth Rock," and after them the "City of Buffalo" and "Western Metropolis," said in their day to have been the world's largest and finest steamboats. But the railroads, then the bane as they were afterwards the salvation of Buffalo, killed the

BUILDERS' EXCHANGE—EXTERIOR VIEW.

passenger business of canal and lake. Buffalo was not much of a manufacturing place then. About all she had was her commerce; and the city fell into a lethargy, in which she was held down by a hard conservatism which had its inception in the time of the 1837 panic, and which would not unbend in the then generation of the moneyed men.

The Lake Fleet.

Commerce increased, though. The stern-wheel craft known as propellers were introduced, with enlarged cargo capacity ; and the lakes were covered with a multitude of fast and graceful sailing vessels. Many of these were rigged as barkantines, and it was a period of high development of seamanship on these inland waters. From season to season their size was increased. When vessels were produced that could carry twenty thousand bushels of wheat, it was considered a wonderfully large load. They could not be built to carry much more until channels had been deepened and widened by the government. Vessel property was very profitable, for grain freights were high, at times going above twenty cents a bushel for wheat. In 1895, when lowest figures on record were reached, wheat was taken from Chicago to Buffalo for less than a cent a bushel.

In former years, all the business of buying and selling grain, chartering vessels, marine insurance, etc., was done on Central Wharf, at the north side of Buffalo River, now covered by railroad freight depots. Although small in comparison with the leviathans of the present, such was the number of the sail vessels that often, after the arrival of a fleet, Buffalo River was completely bridged by them.

An act of the Common Council changed the name of Buffalo Creek to Buffalo River, but, though it sounded better, this did not make more room. The government, however, entered upon the construction of the large outer harbor. After many years' work it is now nearing completion, when the total cost will have been about three millions.

The adoption of the towing system has almost done away with the sailing vessels. The skilled sailors have been succeeded by the deck-hands. In place of the wooden propellers, too, are the great steamships, built on the lines of ocean craft, many of them of steel, and registering nearly up to five thousand tons. These vessels, carrying enormous cargoes, can do so profitably at rates which would be ruinous to the smaller classes of the past.

The United States steamer "Michigan," half a century old or more, and still in commission, was one of the first vessels ever constructed of iron. The parts were made at Pittsburgh, whence they were hauled by wagon to Erie, and there put together. A trim, saucy craft she is to this day, with white decks and shining brass, despite her age and possible infirmities. The first iron vessel actually built at a lake port was the propeller "Merchant," launched from David Bell's yard in Buffalo in the early sixties, and soon followed by the "Philadelphia." These were propellers, with no material change of model or speed from the wooden boats of their kind.

Ship-building was an early industry here. A great many very fine vessels of the various classes have gone out of the Buffalo yards, maintaining the reputation of the port for skill and progressiveness.

BUILDERS' EXCHANGE—INTERIOR VIEW.

The Rebellion.

Icily conservative as Buffalo had become in regard to
business enterprise and public improvements, when the
War of the Rebellion broke out her people were inspired
with patriotism, and nobly performed their duty for the
preservation of the Republic. The regiments which went
from the city all made most honorable records. County
and municipality, and individual citizens as well, gave liber-
ally for the furtherance of the cause. Buffalo's women
worked hard and well to alleviate the condition of the
sick and wounded. Many of the city's worthiest sons fell
in battle or died in the field hospitals.

After the War.

The commerce of the port during the war was very
large, practically all the local energy being concentrated in
it, and much of the available capital invested in it. Hard
times came to the country again in the seventies. The
depression was severely felt by the city, in common with
others, but her superb geographical situation again sus-
tained her; the grain and flour to feed a great part of the
people of the earth had to come through her gateway and
be transferred through her elevators. Commerce was her
mainstay. Her other industries were comparatively insig-
nificant. With that decade a better public spirit began to
be manifest, however, and, at a time when the land was
very cheaply acquired, Buffalo's fine system of parks
was instituted; new public buildings were erected at a
cost of nearly two millions; and, all in all, a more earnest,
reasonable disposition toward progress was shown than
ever before.

Buffalo early sought, but with poor returns, to secure terminals of railroads for which she would be 'something more than a way-station, and which would contribute to make her prosperous. The first venture of this kind was an investment of $200,000 in the stock of the Buffalo & Lake Huron Road, afterwards absorbed by the Grand Trunk. The amount was, practically, a dead loss. After a long breathing spell, and when the luckless deal in the securities of the Canadian line had been about forgotten, another similar but heavier plunge was made. The idea became prevalent that Buffalo ought to be the great oil refining center of the country; that all that was needed to effect that result was a railroad track direct to the wells. "On to Titusville" became the war-cry. A company, the Buffalo & Jamestown, was organized, and the city invested in its stock to the tune of a million. The handsomely printed certificates, which never attained a value other than as souvenirs, repose in the big safe in the Comptroller's office. The road got no further than Jamestown. Reorganized as the Buffalo & Southwestern, it is a leased line of the Erie system. The oil dream evaporated. Still again, and more satisfactorily, the city invested some $700,000 in the Buffalo, New York & Philadelphia, now the Western New York & Pennsylvania. Any further subsidizing of railroad enterprises was prohibited by an amendment to the State Constitution.

YOUNG MENS' CHRISTIAN ASSOCIATION BUILDING.

QUEEN OF THE LAKES.

The New Era.

All these efforts seem to have been ahead of time.
Buffalo was destined to be great, and railroads were to
have a powerful influence on her welfare, but the conditions were not ripe. When the right time did come,
when railroads could no longer afford to ignore Buffalo,
they entered without subsidies, and willing to pay for their
right of way and terminals. With their advent, a number
of strong ones coming almost simultaneously, the new
era for the city began. The purchase of large tracts of
land in the east and southeast parts for the use of the
railroads caused a considerable movement of population
to newer districts, where the people built attractive homes
with the money received for their former holdings. The
real estate business experienced a revival. The new railroads, in the establishment of yards, docks, coal-trestles,
machine-shops, etc., gave employment to a vast number of
men, and furnished a previously unknown stimulus for
manufacturing interests. Buffalo became a manufacturing
as well as a commercial city. Capital from elsewhere
began to appreciate it as a safe place for investment.
Under such circumstances, conservatism was forced to
thaw, in a degree, and in this day is not abnormal. Indeed,
some say that to the healthy conservatism of Buffalo business men is due the fact that Buffalo weathered the panic
of 1893 better than most other cities of the United States.

The census of 1860 gave Buffalo a population of 81,129.

In 1870 it was 117,714, showing an annual increase of only about 3,500 for the ten years. In 1880 the inhabitants numbered 155,134, an annual increase of less than 4,000. Since 1880 the progress of the city has been very remarkable. It is accounted for by the improvement of communication with the coal and oil regions of Pennsylvania, together with the great growth of the West. The Federal census of 1890 showed a population of 255,647; the State census in February, 1892, increased this to 278,796; and an enumeration of the inhabitants by the police in May, 1893, brought the total up to 335,709.

As it is To-day.

Within and backward from the bow formed by the merging shores of Lake Erie and Niagara River, lies the Queen City of the Lakes, the Buffalo of to-day, no larger in territory within the corporate limits than it was many years ago, but vastly increased in population since the turning inward of the tide of her prosperity began about 1880, and immeasurably greater in activity, in industrial pursuits, in wealth, in architecture, in the beauty of her streets, and in the energy of her people. In the last several years the increase of population has been at least twenty thousand per annum; therefore, undoubtedly, at the present time, the city has more than three hundred and fifty thousand inhabitants. Its area is about forty-two square miles, no important addition having been made since 1853, when the boundaries were extended to include Black Rock and other territory. But it has filled up. Ten years ago much of the land within the present limits was unimproved. Where then were bare commons, are now

REAL ESTATE EXCHANGE.

some of the choicest residence streets. A section of the
northeast part of the city, beyond the Parade, then an
open waste, is now built up with the homes of fifty thousand people. The numerical growth has crowded residents
and new-comers toward the suburbs. Fine improvements
of outlying parts, and facilities of rapid transit, have
invited them there.

The city rises gently to a considerable altitude from lake
and river, except that for a short distance along the river
front there is a steep bluff. The only short hills in the
near vicinity are in the North Park and Forest Lawn Cemetery. Main street, running nearly north to the Cold
Spring district, and thence northeast to the city line, divides
the city into what are known as the East and West sides.
The former is more especially the region of railroads, manufactories, and homes of the working people. The West
Side contains the most favored residence districts, although
there are many beautiful places of habitation in the upper
part of the East Side, and at South Buffalo, so called.

The water frontage is about five miles, its length on
the lake and Niagara River being nearly equal. Buffalo
River, as the navigable part of the creek has been chris-
tened, has been made a wide and deep channel for some
two miles from its mouth. This and the Blackwell Canal
and several slips, constitute the inner harbor, where the
bulk of the business of the port is done. The land between Buffalo River and the lake is covered by elevators,
railroad tracks, lumber-yards, coal and ore docks. Fur-
thest up the harbor, the Lehigh Valley Railroad Company
has made great improvement of the lands formerly known
as the Tifft Farm, having by the construction of a series
of canals and trestles, provided the most admirable facil-

ities for its immense coal traffic. On the north side, the Lackawanna Railroad Company occupies the frontage from Main street to the mouth of Buffalo River, where it has a large coal-trestle.

The facilities perfected by the railroads for the storage and expeditious transshipment of coal are gigantic. The docks and coal pockets of the several companies have an average daily shipping capacity of 27,500 tons. Just beyond the eastern city line, in Cheektowaga, are the stocking coal trestle of the Delaware, Lackawanna & Western, with a capacity of over 100,000 tons storage; the Lehigh trestles and stocking plant of 175,000 tons storage capacity; and the Erie stocking plant with storage capacity of 100,000 tons. The Erie is now building at Buffalo a dock and coal trestle a thousand feet long.

Buffalo has thirty-seven grain elevators, with storage capacity aggregating 16,575,000 bushels. Another is in course of construction, to have capacity of 125,000 bushels. Also there are six transfer towers, and eight floating elevators.

The outer harbor, affording a safe haven for vessels, is protected by a breakwater seven thousand six hundred feet long. Its south end is to be nearly reached by a shore arm. When the entire work is finished, a magnificent harbor will be available, and it is expected that docks and piers will line the entire frontage, affording relief to Buffalo River's congested condition.

Along the east side of the city, to and beyond East Buffalo, is an indescribable net-work of railroad tracks. Tracks girdle the city, and widen into new net-works at lower Black Rock. At East Buffalo, the head-quarters of the live stock trade, are the great stock yards of the New York Central, besides numerous extensive manufacturing establishments. These are found in nearly every part of Buffalo where the railroad shipping facilities are convenient. Within the city the New York Central runs frequent trains over a belt line, of which the circuit is fifteen miles. The fare is five cents for any part of or the entire distance.

Buffalo has about one hundred and fifty miles of street railways, under one general management, giving excellent service. The fare is five cents, with privilege of transfer to any line for any continuous ride. Important extensions of the system are projected for the near future. The street railroads have aided greatly in building up the city's border parts. The immense increase of the number of passengers carried within the past few years, is contributory proof of the phenomenal growth of Buffalo within that period. The roads are operated with such care that casualties on the lines have been extremely rare.

Besides by the steam railroads, Buffalo has communication with Niagara Falls and intermediate places by an admirably constructed and equipped electric railway, on which cars are run each way at five-minute intervals. Within the city these cars use the Buffalo Railway Company's tracks to the down-town business district.

Also there are electric railroads to Tonawanda, Lancaster, Williamsville and other near-by towns.

Railroads and Tracks.

Twenty-seven railroads now center at Buffalo, not counting the Connecting Terminal and the Buffalo Creek Transfer roads. The yard facilities for handling the tremendous aggregate of their business are the greatest in the world, the city having within its area of forty-two miles (including the yards of the Delaware, Lackawanna & Western and the West Shore railroads which adjoin the city line on the east), four hundred and fifty miles of tracks. This total will be increased to upwards of six hundred and sixty miles when the terminal improvements and additions already planned by the various roads are completed. At the time of the city's incorporation, in 1832, there were but about one hundred miles of railroads in operation in the United States.

Climate and Health.

Buffalo is one of the healthiest cities of the world, as its very low death rate from year to year has proved. It cannot claim to have nice weather all the year round ; on the other hand, the springs are late. and the summers correspondingly short ; but it seldom knows any notable extreme cf cold or great degree of heat. The summer weather is most delightful, with nights refreshingly cool.

According to the learned official observer at this station, the summers are much cooler than in surrounding cities, due to the fact that the southwest wind, which is the prevailing one, comes from the lake, and that body having a greater capacity of retaining heat than land, the wind is, therefore, much cooler than a land breeze. The fall season is much longer and more uniform than at all other stations of the region, because the lake, which has been heated up during the summer. retains its heat longer than the land, hence the southwest wind, passing over it, brings a warm, moist atmosphere. Although high winds are familiar to Buffalo people, disturbances of a cyclonic

THE GUARANTY BUILDING.

character are almost unknown, and never have been disastrous.

For the first six months of the year, 1895, Buffalo's death rate was 11.67 per 1,000 inhabitants. This was remarkably low—lower than the rate in any other large city of America. The city's Health Department is very vigorously and intelligently conducted. Returns of vital statistics are strictly required, and they are compiled with great care, so that the published averages are as nearly correct as is possible.

Buffalo's Parks.

The city's splendid park system includes 950 acres, and has involved an outlay to the present time of about two million dollars. Designed by Frederick Law Olmsted, and steadily developed since 1870, it has awakened more genuine admiration than any other attraction which Buffalo can present. The chain of parks and parkways nearly encircles the city. Beginning at the confluence of Lake Erie and the Niagara, is the Front, comprising forty-five acres, including the crest of a steep bluff which commands a broad prospect over the water and the Canadian shore. The low land between the Erie Canal and the lake's margin, has been converted into a playground. The elevated territory is increased about seventeen acres by the adjacent open grounds of the military post known as Fort Porter. Formerly there was a real fort here, built some fifty years ago. It consisted of a stone building with moat, drawbridge, and bomb proof covering, the whole surrounded by earthworks. Some years ago the fort proper was burned out, leaving a picturesque ruin which has since disappeared. Eastward from the Front extend the

Prospect Parks, at either side of Niagara street, the ascent of which in that locality has long been known as Prospect Hill. A series of tree-lined avenues one hundred feet wide and of boulevards two hundred feet wide, with double driveways separated by rows of trees, connect the Front with the largest of the parks, the North Park.

This has been laid out with the view of presenting a scene of rural peacefulness. It embraces three hundred and sixty-five acres, forty-six of which form a lake with beautifully shaded banks and numerous small islands laden with shrubbery. A broad sweep of a hundred and fifty acres of undulating turf is known as the Meadow. This is encircled by a road, within which the construction of a cycle path is contemplated. The North Park includes picnic grounds and denser woods, as well as open country, and is laid out with that perfection of art which denotes the hand of the artist. It is adjoined on the west by the two hundred acres of the grounds of the State Hospital for the insane, and on the opposite side by the two hundred and thirty acres of Forest Lawn Cemetery. At this park the beginnings of a zoological collection have been made.

The North Park is connected by another series of parkways with the Parade, a tract of fifty-six acres, consisting mainly of a smooth lawn designed for military drills and popular festivities. Also there is a grove, and a large building which formerly was leased as a restaurant, but is to be converted to a public bath house. The official title of the Parade recently has been changed to Humboldt Park.

In the extreme southeastern part of the city, three parks have been instituted, and are being improved, one of sixty-

ST. PAUL'S EPISCOPAL CHURCH.

two acres at Stony Point, on the Lake Shore ; South Park, of one hundred and fifty acres, and Cazenovia Park, of eighty-two acres. The latter two parks have ponds of about fifteen acres each, and at South Park a Botanic Garden has been established.

The city contemplates an immediate further extension of the park system by the acquisition of lands, including a superb grove, on the bank of Niagara River, at the city's north line.

Water Supply.

No city can have purer or better water than that which is supplied to Buffalo from the strong current near the middle of the Niagara River. It is taken at an inlet pier into a tunnel that conducts the water to the pumping-house on the river bank, whence, for the greater part of the city, it is forced through mains by a pumping plant of several twenty-million and thirty-million gallon engines. A new engine of the latter class has just been put into service, and a second tunnel to the inlet pier is almost completed. On the east side of the city is a great reservoir for supplying the most elevated districts. No other city uses more water *per capita*, and in no other do the people pay less for it,

To the outline given of the topography and natural and acquired advantages of the City of Buffalo, should be added some information of her commerce and industries. To present this within the compressed space available for the purpose, is most difficult, and can only be effectively accomplished with the aid of the eloquence of figures.

World's Sixth Commercial City.

With a season of only about 246 days, in the total tonnage of vessels entered and cleared per year, the port stands behind New York and Chicago alone of American cities, and London, Liverpool and Hamburg of European cities. Buffalo crowds Chicago for the fifth place. The seaports mentioned, it should be remembered, are open the year round. The tonnage of vessels arriving in the District of Buffalo Creek in the season of 1895, aggregated 4,793,338; and of vessels departing, 4,819,085—a grand total of 9,612,423 tons.

Greatest in These.

In handling flour and wheat, Buffalo is the first city in the world. During the year 1895, there were received here by lake alone, 8,971,740 barrels of flour, 47,256,005 bushels of wheat, 37,579,311 of corn, 22,231,271 of oats, 10,958,229 of barley, and 871,612 of rye. Reducing flour to wheat, the grand total of 163,755,128 bushels of grain is obtained. Lake receipts of numerous other articles, such as flax-seed, shingles, pig iron, ore, copper, etc., were also very large.

Also Buffalo is the first city in the world in the distribution of coal. In 1880 the shipments from the port were less than 500,000 tons. In 1895 they aggregated 2,620,768 tons.

Other important items of export by lake included 562,618 barrels of cement, 669,078 barrels or salt, and 1,097,767 barrels of sugar.

Second to Chicago alone as a lumber market, the receipts of 1895 at Buffalo and Tonawanda were 632,-051,476 feet.

THE SOLDIERS' AND SAILORS' MONUMENT.

Of the enormous movement of various commodities from Buffalo by rail, definite figures are not readily obtainable.

Live Stock Trade.

At East Buffalo the vast trade in live stock is centered. The yards comprise about seventy-five acres, of which some twenty-five afford merely transfer facilities for the Erie, Lehigh Valley and Lackawanna Railroads, while the remainder form the model sales-yards of the New York Central. In 1895 the receipts for sale in these yards were 10,082 cars of cattle, 12,983 cars of hogs, and 11,750 cars of sheep and lambs. The totals received both for sale and for through shipment were 795,850 head of cattle, 3,983,616 hogs, 2,685,700 sheep and lambs. The stock slaughtered in the city during the year included 69,080 head of cattle, 1,437,120 hogs, and 1,041,000 sheep. The horse market is said to be now the largest in the country. Some five thousand more were sold in 1895 than in the previous year, but largely at what seemed ruinously low prices, attributable to the substitution of electricity as street railroad motive power, and the free use of the bicycle. The year's receipts of horses at East Buffalo were 96,500.

What has been thus tersely said of the commercial interests of the Queen City of the Lakes, will serve to indicate their grand magnitude, and will also convey an inference of the great number of people to whom they give employment.

The city has twenty-two commercial banks with aggregate capital of $5,850,000, and surplus of $4,626,785; also four savings banks, with assets of about $38,000,000.

Manufactures.

The Federal census of 1890, showed for Buffalo the largest percentage of increase of manufactories in the decade. At present they are said to number about three thousand five hundred, with probably a hundred thousand operatives. Although not an iron center, there are large blast furnaces at Tonawanda and Buffalo, and within the city proper the manufacture of light and heavy machinery is an important industry; also the making of agricultural implements. Naturally, much work for railroads is done in factories here, where cars, car-wheels and axles are made, and locomotives built and repaired. The Wagner Car Company's shops employ from fifteen hundred to two thousand hands. The Lake Erie Engine Works, which turn out both engines and boilers, have a lathe and boring machine, which, at the time they were set up, were said to be the largest of their kind in the world. The barbette armor-plates for the war-ship "New York" were brought here to be finished with these appliances. The flour mills of the city in 1895, produced 1,354,523 barrels. Among principal products of local industries are mill and sugar-making apparatus, wall-paper, harness trimmings and malleable iron goods, leather, soap, etc., to which are added minor articles of trade in almost endless variety. The malting interest is very large. Of ale and beer, made by upwards of twenty breweries, the annual output approximates three-quarters of a million barrels. Of the lithographing and show-printing business, Buffalo is a center.

THE BUFFALO LIBRARY BUILDING.

Lake Passenger Traffic.

Within three years a substantial revival of passenger business on the lakes has been witnessed, due to the enterprise of sanguine projectors of boats which afford all the comforts and elegancies of a great metropolitan hotel. The Cleveland & Buffalo Line has just added to its fleet a sumptuously appointed great side-wheel steamer, named the "City of Buffalo." The Northern Steamship Company has in commission between Buffalo and Duluth the monster steel steamships "North West" and "North Land," each of four thousand five hundred tons. These ships carry no freight, and are claimed to have a speed of over twenty-four miles an hour.

Protection of Crossings.

Before the community awoke to realization of the evil, the railroads had established a great number of crossings of the streets of Buffalo at grade. Its seriousness was in time, however, made plain to the public mind by a constant succession of painful disasters to human life and limb, and much vexatious delay of traffic. Manifestly the only remedy was to require the railroads to elevate or depress their tracks at the crossings where the danger and inconvenience were most pronounced. The appointment of a Commission of citizens was obtained, who devised a general plan for the abatement of the trouble. A long and at times discouraging struggle ensued, the railroads opposing the enterprise with all their power, and employing all the tactics of obstruction that ingenious counsel could invent. The citizens, however, succeeded in securing for the Commission coercive powers from the Legistature, despite the railroad influence. The New York Central Company was the first to come to terms and sign a contract for its part of the proposed work. The others, one by one, surrendered to the inevitable, until now all are harmonized, and the vast undertaking is fairly under way, with an equitable adjustment between the railroads and the city of the cost of the improvements, which, in the end, will amount to several millions.

The present completed feature of the scheme is the great viaduct by which Michigan street is carried over the New York Central tracks and the Hamburg Canal. The tunnel under Main street and subway through the Terrace, for tracks used by New York Central and Michigan Central trains, are far advanced at this writing.

A Cosmopolitan City.

Buffalo's population is cosmopolitan, with large elements from Germany, the Polish Provinces and Italy. Probably one-third of the people are of German birth or parentage. To its Germans the city is indebted for much of its material prosperity. Many Irish people came here with the tide of immigration. They have become so thoroughly Americanized as to have practically lost foreign distinctiveness. The Polish colony probably numbers fifty thousand souls, at the least. They came here poor, but with an instinct for thrift, and have developed a most ardent ambition to own their own homes. They have built great churches, and many have become substantial property holders. As a class they are law-abiding, patriotic, useful members of society. The Italians, although not so numerous, form a considerable colony, with many estimable and well-to-do citizens.

THE GROSVENOR LIBRARY BUILDING.

These and other representatives from foreign countries, who have made Buffalo their home, have a great number of civic and religious organizations, with many imposing church, school, and other edifices.

Home of Presidents.

Buffalo has had the honor of furnishing from her citizenship two Presidents of the United States of America.

Millard Fillmore, born in Cayuga County, N. Y., on January 7, 1800, came on foot to Buffalo in 1821, arriving here an entire stranger, with four dollars in his pocket. He obtained permission to study in a lawyer's office, supporting himself by severe drudgery in teaching school and assisting the postmaster. In 1823 he began practice in Aurora, Erie County. In 1830 he returned to Buffalo. His political life began in 1828, when he was elected to the State Legislature by the anti-Masonic party. After serving four terms in Congress, he retired from that body in 1842. In 1844 he was nominated for Governor, but was defeated by Silas Wright. In June, 1848, he was nominated by the Whig national convention for Vice-President, on the ticket with Zachary Taylor, and was elected. The death of Gen. Taylor, on the 9th of July, 1850, elevated Mr. Fillmore to the Presidency, from which he retired March 4, 1853. He died in Buffalo, March 8, 1874. His grave and monument are in Forest Lawn. The house facing Niagara Square at Delaware avenue, which was long Mr. Fillmore's residence, still stands, although enlarged by extensions and in other respects changed. On the Delaware avenue side is the bow window, his favorite sitting place, in which the stately form of the ex-President was for years familiar to passers-by.

In 1855, Grover Cleveland, who was born in Caldwell, Essex County, New Jersey, on the 18th of March, 1837, on his way west in quest of something to do, stopped at Black Rock to visit his uncle, rugged and able Lewis F. Allen, who died a few years ago at an advanced age. Mr. Allen induced him to remain, and aid him in the compilation of a volume of the "American Herd Book." For six weeks' service at this work he gave the youth $60. Grover stayed here. In 1855 he entered the law office of the prominent firm of Rogers, Bowen & Rogers as a clerk. In 1859 he was admitted to the bar. His first public office was that of Assistant District Attorney, to which he was appointed in January, 1863. In 1865 he was the Democratic candidate for District Attorney of Erie County, but was defeated by his personal friend, the brilliant Lyman K. Bass. He then entered into partnership with Isaac V. Vanderpoel (who, by the way, was one of the most genial and popular of men), and in 1869 became a member of the firm of Laning, Cleveland & Folsom. The junior member of this firm, Oscar Folsom, was the father of the present Lady of the White House. She was born in this city, in 1864, and graduated from Buffalo's High School. Elected Sheriff of the county in 1870, at the expiration of his term Mr. Cleveland retired from office, and from active politics for a long time. Some who were dissatisfied with his administration while Sheriff, now averred that he was politically dead. They were destined to witness a startling resurrection. In 1881 he was elected Mayor of Buffalo. Since then Governor of New York and twice President of the United States, his phenomenal career in public life is familiar to the world. Wilson S. Bissell, recently a member of President Cleveland's cabinet, is a resident of Buf-

THE MOONEY-BRISBANE BUILDING.

falo, and after 1874 was long his law partner. He is now
the head of the law firm of Bissell, Sicard, Bissell & Carey.
To the time of his removal to Washington, Mr. Cleveland
was listed as a confirmed bachelor, but on June 2, 1886, in
the White House, he married Frances Folsom. At the
northwest corner of Main and Swan streets stands the
building in which for a good many years Grover Cleveland maintained his law office and kept bachelor's hall.

"Father of Greenbacks."

Another citizen of Buffalo who has a more than national
reputation, is the Hon. Elbridge Gerry Spaulding, who,
although far beyond man's ordinary allotment of years, is
still in active business life. His home is at the southeast
corner of Main and Goodell streets, opposite Music Hall.
The advance of business and social interests has ruth-
lessly encroached upon the privacy of that neighborhood.

Born in Summer Hill, Cayuga County, N. Y., on February 24, 1809, he studied law in Batavia and Attica, was
admitted to the bar in 1836, and removed to Buffalo. In
the same year he was appointed City Clerk. He was
elected Alderman in 1841, and Mayor in 1847; was a
member of the State Legislature of 1848; a member of
the Thirty-first Congress; Treasurer of the State of New
York, 1854–5; and member of the Thirty-sixth and Thirty-
seventh Congresses. During his last term in Congress, Mr.
Spaulding was a member of the Ways and Means Committee, and chairman of the sub-committee that was
entrusted with the duty of preparing legislative measures.
The result was the presentation and passage of the Green-
back or Legal-Tender Act, and the National Currency

Bank Bill. Both of these were drawn by Mr. Spaulding. They were offered and urged as war measures, and, says one of his biographers, "are claimed to be the best financial system that was ever conceived or adopted by any government. Mr. Spaulding is entitled to the credit of formulating these measures and securing their adoption. By reason of his connection with this important legislation, he has been called the ' Father of Greenbacks.' "

Through the larger part of his life he has been engaged in the business of banking, accumulating large wealth. With some Buffalonians a favorite pastime is guessing at the number of Mr. Spaulding's millions.

View of the City.

Very long ago Buffalo became a beautiful city of homes, but very long its light was hidden. The architecture of its down-town business part, originally of the plainest description, became shabby with the passage of time. Owners of many buildings, neither attractive without nor convenient within, were disinclined to replace them as long as they could command fair rentals. Others of similar class were on land leased for long periods, and destined to stay until the leases expired. Not a few of these yet occupy very desirable sites; but the new architectural era is causing their gloomy rooms to become tenantless, and they will soon have to " get off the earth," for the ground they cover is too valuable to be encumbered with structures without profit. Buffalo was badly advertised by her principal business district, as she is to-day by the inconsequential appearance of her railroad stations and their generally forlorn environment. A multitude of peo-

THE HOTEL IROQUOIS.

ple *en route* through the city, while waiting for trains, have walked a few blocks and then returned to the shelter of the railroad waiting-rooms, prepared to spread the report that Buffalo was not worth seeing. All ignorant were they of the miles upon miles of beautiful drives and parks, and the myriad of elegant residences, with their exquisitely kept grounds, that lay beyond the barrier of dingy stores and warehouses of the style of sixty years agone.

A great change, however, already has been wrought, and the transformation steadily proceeds. No one can now stray many blocks from the railroad stations without becoming impressed with the evidences of the city's dignity and importance.

View some of the products of the new genius of enterprise that has made its abode here; and there can be no more convenient starting place than the commanding position of the Builders' Exchange, from which the results of recent investments of many millions in the safest of all property—land and buildings—may be seen in a single glance. First, however, something of the Exchange building itself, and the association which owns it:

Buffalo Builders' Association Exchange.

The Buffalo Builders' Exchange is the outgrowth of a movement begun in 1867, when, on February 6th, in response to a call by the late Joseph Churchyard, representatives of twenty-two firms met and resolved upon the formation of the "Builders' Association of Buffalo." The first officers, elected on February 19th of that year, were: Amos Morgan, President; Henry Rumrill, Vice-

President; J. H. Tilden, Corresponding Secretary; C. S. Chapin, Joseph Churchyard, John Walls, William I. Williams and John Briggs, Curators. This organization, twenty years later, became a member of the National Association of Builders, and it was then deemed advisable to make eligible to membership not only masons and carpenters, but workmen in all branches of the trade, as well as dealers in builders' supplies. To carry out this plan, the local association was incorporated as the Builders' Association Exchange, in the month of April, 1888.

There are two classes of membership of the Exchange : Corporate membership, admitting only those who are engaged in the mechanical trades necessary to the erection of a building; and non-corporate membership, admitting firms or individuals carrying on in their own names branches of business subsidiary to the mechanical trades represented in the corporation. The corporate members, who are the stockholders, have the management of the Exchange. The non-corporate members have the privileges of the Exchange and reading-room.

The first headquarters were in the Jewett building, on Washington street, opened on May 1st, 1888, and the long-considered plan of daily meetings was put into successful operation, with a superintendent in charge. Soon it was evident that the importance of the Exchange demanded better facilities, and the subject of a building to be owned by the association was broached, and immediately became popular. On March 10th, 1891, a fire cleared the lot at the northwest corner of Court and Pearl streets, bringing the land into market at favorable terms, and it was secured without delay—an admirable site, of which already the value has greatly increased.

THE ELLICOTT SQUARE.

For the purpose of buying the lot and erecting a building, it was necessary to form a new association, to be known as the Builders' Exchange Association, as a joint stock company, with capital stock of $75,000, the membership being drawn exclusively from the old corporation. On July 13th, 1891, ground was broken ; on May 1st, 1892, the structure was so far advanced that it was partially occupied, the Exchange finding temporary quarters on the first floor ; on July 1st, it took permanent possession of the second floor. The lot cost $45,000 and the structure $130,000. The frontage on Court street is fifty-one feet six inches, and on Pearl street eighty-six feet six inches.

Constructed of stone, brick and iron, the building is strictly fire-proof. It has seven stories above the basement, the ground floor being four feet above the sidewalk. The basement and first story are of red Medina sandstone, backed with brick laid in cement. The walls above are faced with pressed brick, with cut stone trimmings of bed-rock Prentiss brown stone from Lake Superior, this being the first building in Buffalo in which this material was employed. The several floors and roof are constructed throughout with steel girders and beams, and hollow brick arches laid in cement.

The design may with propriety be designated as Italian renaissance, the first story being Tuscan, the second and third Roman Doric, the fourth and fifth Ionic, and the sixth and seventh Corinthian. It is in the strictest sense an office building. Every room is well lighted, and every convenience is provided. At night the entire building is illuminated by electricity. The second floor is occupied exclusively by the Builders' Exchange, for its business office, board room and assembly room. Part of the first floor is used for a permanent exhibition of building materials and supplies.

Stand now where the Builders' Exchange corners, and look north, south, east and west. To the north, in the near vicinity, on Pearl street, are other large structures for business purposes. At Mohawk street, and fronting thereon,, and on Pearl and Genesee streets as well, is the fine four-story brick building of the city's Central Department of the Young Men's Christian Association. It was erected in 1884, and is admirably fitted for the social and physical benefit of the great number of the members, as well as their spiritual improvement. Across the way, at Genesee and Pearl streets, is the Central Presbyterian Church, a large edifice of stone, which for more than a generation was familiarly known as Dr. Lord's Church; and the old people in Buffalo call it so still, although its long-time pastor and powerful preacher, the Rev. Dr. John C. Lord, years ago closed his earthly labors. Still north, and to its termination at Tupper street, Pearl street is in the period of transition, residences becoming boarding-houses, and these gradually disappearing before the march of business. Its near neighbor, Franklin street, next parallel to the west, is in similar process of change, although the upper part is yet entirely lined with homes of an elegant class. Between Niagara and Tupper streets, Franklin was formerly occupied by many doctors of the well-to-do grade, but "Doctors' Row" has moved over to Delaware avenue. Franklin, in time, is sure to become an important business thoroughfare.

Pearl street, a few years ago, gloomy and ill-paved, below Court street, was in the public eye only a place important for the back doors and delivery wagons of the Main

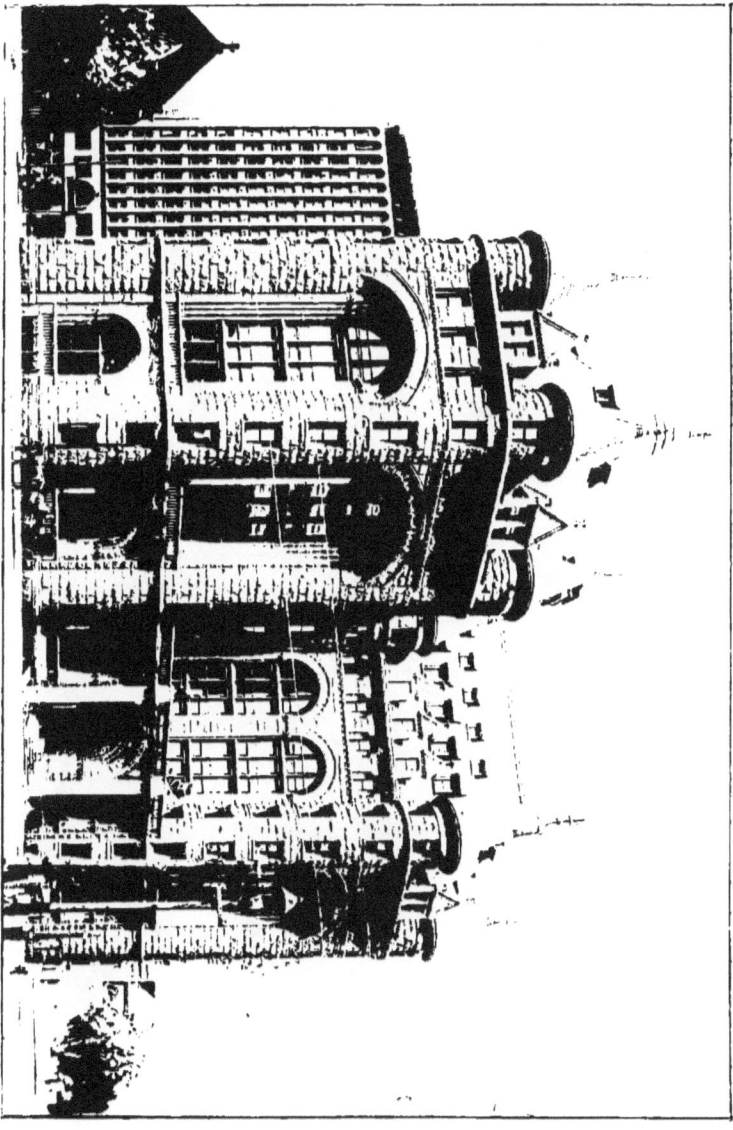

ERIE COUNTY SAVINGS BANK BUILDING.

street stores ; but a radical change in its future has come about, as anyone seeking to buy property there now would soon be made to comprehend. The first of Buffalo's tall buildings of structural steel was built on this street ; other and greater ones have gathered on it ; and, as a result, there has been a very strong rise in the value of its real estate. On the west side of Pearl, between Court and Eagle streets, is the splendid new Real Estate Exchange. At Church street is the towering Guaranty building ; and at Swan street is the pioneer of this style of construction, the Dun building.

Court street, from Main street to Niagara Square, is a very broad and fine avenue. Looking west from Pearl, and past the buildings of the High School and the Women's Christian Association, Niagara Square is in sight, formed by the intersection of four streets — a large expanse of white asphalt pavement, framed with the sward of pointed miniature parks. Formerly, Niagara Square was surrounded by the mansions of some of the most substantial citizens of earlier Buffalo, but its important buildings now belong to semi-public institutions—the Women's Educational and Industrial Union, the Women's Christian Association, the Working Boys' Home. For the latter, on the site it now occupies, a large and handsome new building is soon to be provided.

Looking up Court street, which ends at Main, the eye rests on the graceful monument to Buffalo's soldiers and sailors of the Civil War, which rises from Lafayette Square to a height of nearly a hundred feet, forming a fine picture with the red tile-roofs of the ornate Buffalo Library Building in the background.

Before going further in the quest of what Buffalo can show that is architecturally impressive, a few details of some features which have been given passing mention :

Real Estate Exchange.

Built of steel, and a nearly white terra cotta, the building of the Buffalo Real Estate Exchange is of ten stories and basement. Designed to concentrate the offices of the real estate men, it gives room to other interests as well. The interior is of fire-proof tile, marble and iron. The contract for this building was let on June 29th, 1895 ; the excavation was begun on July 15th, and the placing of the steel work on September 29th. The banquet with which the formal opening was observed, was served on the 24th of April, 1896. The time taken in the construction of this great modern office building, complete in all its particulars, was one hundred and seventy-eight working days. This, for rapidity, is said to be unequaled in Buffalo, and rarely equaled anywhere. The land was appraised at $225,000, and the edifice cost $500,000. No other organization of real estate men in the country, if in the entire world, has put up a building to compare with this one. The Real Estate Exchange in New York City even occupies rented quarters.

The main entrance to the building is in keeping with its otherwise imposing facade. It is flanked by twelve white marble columns, supporting a richly decorated arch. This entrance is sixteen feet wide and thirty-two feet high. The Exchange room has an arched ceiling, rising to a height of thirty-five feet, supported at either end by four massive marble columns. Rich marble wainscoting, pil-

LIVE STOCK EXCHANGE.

lars and cornices, add to the decorative effect. It is the finest Real Estate Exchange room in the land. Here the real estate dealers meet daily at the 'Change hour, and the judicial sales of the city and county are held.

The Guaranty Building.

This splendid structure, at the southwest corner of Pearl and Church streets, is owned by the Chicago Guaranty Construction Company, and finished in the spring of 1896. Its frontage on Pearl street is ninety-five feet, and on Church one hundred and sixteen feet. It is thirteen stories high, besides a finished basement. Great claims are made of the perfection of this building as a sample of the modern style of steel construction. Plain in its grand outlines, its dark red terra cotta covering is profusely decorated. The foundation of the building, which rests upon steel beams set crosswise in a bed of cement, was made with extreme care and at large cost. Within, the plan is very convenient and compact, with every room well lighted. The corridors are paved with marble mosaic, and wainscoted with pink marble from Tennessee. The interior wood-work is of oak and Mexican mahogany. The elevator shafts, and the stairways above the wainscoting, as well as all outer court walls, are faced with white enameled brick. There is much rich bronze-work, wrought to correspond in design with that of the terra cotta ornamentation of the exterior.

The cost of this truly magnificent office building was six hundred thousand dollars, exclusive of the price of the land.

St. Paul's Church.

Opposite the Guaranty Building, on Pearl street, is
St. Paul's, made the cathedral church of the Episcopal
Diocese of Western New York by the late Bishop Arthur
Cleveland Coxe. Occupying the triangular space bounded
by Pearl, Church and Erie streets, its rear is toward Main
street, and visitors often wonder that it was so placed.
This church has long been noted as one of the most beautiful examples of ecclesiastical architecture in the country.
Designed by Upjohn, it was built in 1850, but its singularly
graceful spire, which reaches an altitude of two hundred
and sixty-eight feet, was completed more than twenty years
later. The entire structure is of red sandstone. Its pre-
decessor on the same site was the first Episcopal church
in Buffalo—a frame affair which was moved to an east
side street where it yet stands.

On the west side of Pearl street, just south of the Guaranty Building, an elegant and commodious fire-proof par-
ish house for St. Paul's congregation is about to be built.

The Soldiers' Monument.

The breathing-space known as Lafayette Square is
bounded by Main, Clinton, Washington and Lafayette
streets. The surroundings are of the finest. To the south
is the splendid facade of the Mooney-Brisbane Building.
To the east is the Library Building and the head of Broadway, which wide avenue stretches far away to the eastern
city line. To the north is the old Lafayette street church
—which, no doubt, must soon make way for some lofty
and palatial edifice for business use—and the German

BANK OF BUFFALO.

Insurance Building, which corners at Lafayette and Main streets. That was the first building here of the iron and glass front style of construction. The church alluded to—it succeeded another which was destroyed by fire nearly half a century ago—was but recently abandoned by the congregation, upon the completion of a more modern and far more beautiful structure on Elmwood avenue, some three miles away from the old site. Very few of the early churches remain where they were originally instituted. Pressed by the enlargement of the business district, they have moved "up-town."

Buffalo has too few small interior parks. Lafayette Square is a delight and of inestimable value to the people, but made so chiefly by its environment, and by its noble monument to the city's soldiers and sailors. This memorial was unveiled on the Fourth of July in 1884. It was the outcome of eight years of agitation, started and kept up by an organization known as the Ladies' Monument Association. Originally the idea was to build a memorial arch over Delaware avenue where it enters Niagara Square, and the ceremony of breaking ground beside the Millard Fillmore residence was actually performed with appropriate ceremonies; but public opinion dissented, and as the city was to pay for the work, public opinion had its way—in this case properly, for surely there could be no more fit place for the monument than where it stands.

The sum of forty thousand dollars was appropriated, and in due season the creation of granite and bronze was set up and dedicated. Originally its height was eighty-five feet. Within a few years it began to perceptibly settle out of plumb. The sub-foundation had been improperly laid by the contractor for that part of the work. The entire structure had to be taken down, which was no idle task. A great derrick was rigged, by which the massive sections of the monument were lowered safely to the ground. The opportunity was now taken to improve the base plan by constructing a platform with copings and stairway approaches. With this improvement, when the monument was again reared, its height was increased to about a hundred feet.

As has been well said, "it is a strikingly beautiful monument, filled with artistic sentiment bearing directly upon its purpose, and adorning in the highest manner its conspicuous position in the busiest part of the city." About the base are four bronze figures representing the infantry, the cavalry, the artillery, and the navy. These were designed by Casper Buberl, as was also the admirable bas-relief, picturing the departure of troops, which encircles the column. The monument is surmounted by a colossal statue, cut out of the granite, which idealizes Buffalo.

The space about the monument has green turf, flowerbeds and broad walks. The Buffalo Historical Society has had mounted and placed in the Square two old cannons and a mortar which did service in the war of 1812. One of the cannons a few years ago was dug out of the clay bank of Niagara River.

Buffalo Library Association.

Under the name of the Young Men's Association, since changed to the more appropriate one, this institution was founded in the year 1836, with the purpose of accumulating and maintaining a circulating library. It still lends

BANK OF COMMERCE.

books to members who pay the small amount of annual dues, but its sphere has substantially widened, and it now has a comprehensive reference library, with many volumes that are rare and almost invaluable ; also extensive collections of manuscripts and autographs. After "rooming about " for several years, the library was settled in the old American Hotel building, where it thrived apace. Winter courses of lectures were given ; art exhibitions and entertainments were encouraged. To be president of the Young Men's Association became an honor, considered nearly equal with that of being mayor of the city. With the flight of time, the ambition of the association enlarged ; its spirit of enterprise quickened, and in 1864 entered into a definite plan which the citizens encouraged with generous financial aid. The Association acquired title to the St. James Hotel and St. James Hall, which covered the site of the present Iroquois Hotel. St. James Hall—successor to the ancient Eagle Street Theater—was long the city's largest place of public gathering. Within its walls the remains of Abraham Lincoln lay in state, while the funeral escort rested here in 1865. The Association had the interior of the hotel building remodeled for the uses of the library, and brought under the same roof the Buffalo Historical Society, the Academy of Fine Arts, and the Society of Natural Sciences.

In this habitation the library remained until its growth and value became such that it seemed tempting fate to much longer keep the collection, and the treasures of the other societies, in a building that was not fire-proof. In 1883 another appeal was made to the citizens, with the result that a fund of $117,000 was contributed. With this sum on hand, the Association embarked in the building project of which the beautiful structure facing Lafayette Square was the outcome. After the completion of the new city and county buildings on Franklin and Delaware streets, the historic "Old Court-house," on Washington street, the old "New Court-house," on Clinton and Ellicott streets, and the old jail on Broadway (formerly Batavia street) were abandoned. The Association secured the land. The site is not now considered the most favorable for a building where quiet is a desirable condition; but the building itself could hardly show to as fine advantage, and to so many stranger visitors, in any other locality. The work was finished in 1887, at a cost of $338,000.

The very elegant gothic structure is of red stone, red brick and iron—as nearly fire-proof as possible. Its picturesque appearance cannot be adequately described in words. The first intention was to build the walls entirely of stone, but the cost was ascertained to be too great. The handsome interior of the first story is arranged to meet a great modern library's every requirement. The present number of books is over eighty thousand, and of pamphlets ten thousand,

Retaining the property on Main, Eagle and Washington streets, the Association caused the old library building (formerly the St. James Hotel) to be reconstructed and enlarged for hotel use, and it was opened as The Richmond. Its career was very brief, ending with the dreadful conflagration, in which The Richmond and St. James Hall were swept away. On the land thus cleared the Buffalo Library Association has since erected the magnificent Hotel Iroquois. The institution now is heavily incumbered with debt; it has a greater load than it should be made to carry, but there is no fear that Buffalo will ever let it break down.

THE BOARD OF TRADE.

Society of Natural Sciences.

In the basement of the Buffalo Library Building, the Society of Natural Sciences, organized in 1861, has its quarters. Here may be seen a fine collection of mineral specimens, illustrating the local geology, and fossils that fairly represent the different periods; a good lithological exhibit, obtained chiefly from Europe; large ornithological and entomological collections; a very complete herbarium, the work of the late Judge George W. Clinton; a small but fine lot of pottery from Chiriqui, Central America; and the Riggs' collection of mound-builders' pottery. These and other treasures which have been accumulated, and to which additions are made frequently, constitute an exhibition alike valuable and exceedingly interesting Associated with the Society of Natural Sciences are the Naturalists' Field Club, the Microscopical Society, the Buffalo Electrical Society and the Engineers' Society.

Academy of Fine Arts.

This institution, which dates from 1862, has fine rooms in the building, with excellent light and arrangement for its gallery, in which periodical exhibitions of a high order of merit are held. The Academy is the owner of numerous pictures of much merit, representing such leading American artists as Wyant, T. Moran, E. Moran, Thompson, E. Wood Perry, Beard, Gifford, McEntee, and others. It also possesses notable collections of engravings and etchings. Connected with the Academy is a prosperous Art School.

Buffalo Historical Society.

The third floor of the Library Building is devoted to
the use of the Buffalo Historical Society, which has a
library of some ten thousand volumes and many thou-
sands of pamphlets, besides a large museum of relics and
curios, mostly related to the history of Western New
York. The Society has issued a number of extremely
valuable publications, and has labored with great industry
to preserve the history of this part of the country, and
especially of its early Indian inhabitants. Through its
efforts the remains of Red Jacket, and other chiefs,
were re-interred in Forest Lawn Cemetery, and a monument with fine bronze statue of the famous red orator
erected.

The Grosvenor Library.

Across Broadway from the Buffalo Library building is
the Buffalo Savings Bank building, in the second story of
which, from 1870, for twenty-five years the Grosvenor
Library was placed. This institution was founded upon
a gift of forty thousand dollars from the late Seth Grosvenor, of which ten thousand was to be applied to the purchase of a lot, the remainder to be preserved as a fund of
which the interest should be used for the acquirement of
books. The city accepted the gift, appointed a board of
trustees to manage the library, and has annually appropriated five thousand dollars for its running expenses. The
original plan was to maintain purely a reference library,

MASONIC TEMPLE.

and there has been no deviation from it. No books may be taken away from the rooms. Their use is free to all orderly comers. In time the need of a home of its own for the Grosvenor Library became pressing.

The city, in 1865, deeded to the library the old "Mohawk Street Market" property—now the site of the Young Men's Christian Association building—the sale of which added a considerable fund to the original nest-egg. The money was kept invested until further increased materially by interest, and until, in the belief of the trustees, the building enterprise long projected could be no longer deferred wisely. A lot at the corner of Franklin and Edward streets, with quiet and pleasant surroundings, was bought, and the building erected in which the Grosvenor Library is now permanently housed. The building has a basement and one high story, with a large tower in which there is a pleasant room, over which is an observatory intended for the reception of an astronomical telescope. Of stone, brick and iron, the building is generally attractive, and especially so within, where the light and arrangements for undisturbed study or research are practically perfect. The number of volumes on the shelves at this time is about forty thousand.

The German Young Men's Association has a library of about eight thousand volumes in its rooms in the first story of the Music Hall building, and the Catholic Institute has one of some six thousand volumes. Of literary and kindred societies, Buffalo has her full quota. Of musical, social, professional and benevolent organizations, the name is legion.

Mooney-Brisbane Building.

Facing Lafayette Square from the south, this great and magnificent building presents a frontage of imposing beauty, while its Main street and Washington street facades are hardly less effective. Seven stories high, and of the classic renaissance architecture, its materials are steel, brick, cut stone and terra cotta. The frontage on Main and Washington streets is one hundred and eighty feet, and on Clinton street two hundred feet. The cost was about half a million. The building was completed in 1895. The construction is such that the entire first floor can be used as one great store. The second floor has an arrangement of eighteen bazaars, all fronting on a court fifty feet wide. The stories above are divided into offices, of which there are thirty-six on each floor.

The Iroquois Hotel.

With frontage of a hundred feet on Main and Washington streets, and two hundred feet on Eagle street, the Iroquois Hotel, the property of the Buffalo Library Association, is an absolutely fire-proof structure, eight stories high, built of brown stone, brick and iron. Imposing without, it is beautiful and complete within, lacking nothing that is required in a strictly modern hotel of the first-class. Its cost was upwards of eight hundred thousand dollars, and it has accommodation for five hundred guests. It was opened to the public in 1889.

CITY AND COUNTY HALL.

Ellicott Square.

Joseph Ellicott, founder of Buffalo, the far-sighted man "who wrought with a magnificent hope," will not be forgotten, for in his memory a vast, impressive creation has been named, a monument of the most effective, enduring character. He planned Buffalo; foresaw and predicted its ultimate grandeur. It is fit that his name should be honored.

He was born in Bucks County, Pennsylvania, on November 1, 1760. His father, also named Joseph, immigrated from England, and built the mills which gave the name to Ellicott's Mills, Maryland. His brother, Andrew, was a professor of mathematics at West Point, where he died in 1820. The elder Ellicotts were Quakers, but parted from that sect in order to serve in the Continental Army during the American Revolution. The depreciation of the Continental money made the father a poor man, therefore the younger Joseph worked on a farm, and received but a meager education; but in later years he had a great thirst for knowledge, and studied assiduously. He acquired the science of surveying, and was engaged in important works, including the laying out of the city of Washington, the nation's new capital. In the year 1797, he began the survey of the Holland Land Company's purchase. He was chosen for the task as the most competent surveyor obtainable. He first surveyed the company's lands in Pennsylvania, then traced the southern line of Lake Ontario, the Niagara River, and the border of Lake Erie to the Pennsylvania line. In the spring of 1798, he brought from Philadelphia a hundred and fifty men to aid in the gigantic task of the division of the Holland purchase into townships. The whole survey was completed before the year 1800, and his work was so satisfactory that Ellicott was appointed agent for the Holland Company, with office at Batavia. "Even when his views were not the most immediately remunerative to the company," one of his biographers has said, "his ideas were based upon an almost prophetic perception of the future growth of Western New York."

Mr. Ellicott is said to have been a generous and a just as well as a strong man. The close of his remarkably active life was most sorrowful. "His health began to fail in 1824, and a deep melancholy settled upon him. He consulted eminent physicians in New York, and, yielding to their advice, entered the lunatic asylum at Bloomingdale for treatment. His condition did not improve, and the unfortunate man ended his misery by suicide, August 19th, 1826." The Indians did not like Ellicott, regarding him as the chief promoter of immigration by white men. It is related that he and Red Jacket once met in the Tonawanda swamp, and sat together on a log. Presently the chief exclaimed, "Move along, Joe." Ellicott complied. The request was repeated several times, until Ellicott's next move would have been into the mire. Looking for an explanation, he was thus addressed by the Seneca: "That is the way the white man treats us. He first says, 'Move along a little,' and then 'a little more,' and when we have moved as far as we can, he shoves us out of the world." This "historical note" prefaced the Ellicott Square Company's prospectus: "In 1797, Joseph Ellicott, agent of the Holland Land Company, laid out the village of New Amsterdam, now the City of Buffalo. His plan was, in a measure, copied from that of Washington,

WOMEN'S EDUCATIONAL AND INDUSTRIAL UNION.

D. C., the peculiar feature being the radiation of streets from the center of the city, and from other principal points. He reserved for his residence and private estate the most desirable location in the village, which was on the east side of Main street, extending from Swan street to Eagle street, and his mansion was intended to look up and down Main street, and also to look down Niagara street, Church street and Erie street, which radiate from Main street at this point. Subsequently, for about one hundred years, his heirs and their successors retained title to that part of the property between Swan street and South Division street, extending from Main street to Washington street, and this has therefore been known, and is still known, as Ellicott Square."

Ellicott Square, said to be the largest office building in the world, is as graceful in every outline as its immensity is majestic. Everywhere is beauty. Its vast size perhaps is not at once appreciated by the unaccustomed eye, for it is so high that its horizontal lines may seem shortened; and it is so long that its height may appear dwarfed. But study it from different points, and the perfection of its proportions will be realized. Its frontages on Main and Washington streets are two hundred and forty feet, those on Swan and South Division streets two hundred feet. It is of ten stories. The height of the crest line from the sidewalk is one hundred and forty-four feet. In the center of the building is a grand court, seventy by a hundred and ten feet, roofed with glass above the second story. This great roof has no other support than at the sides. The frame of the building is of steel, the walls of terra cotta of pearl-gray.

On the ground floor are forty stores. There are six

hundred offices and suites of offices, making a total of about twelve hundred rooms.

In the construction of the building were used five thousand five hundred and fifty tons of steel, twelve thousand tons of fire-proofing, a thousand tons of plaster, six thousand barrels of cement, four hundred thousand square feet of maple flooring, two hundred and fifty tons of glass, one hundred and twenty-five tons of sash-weights, fifteen miles of pipe of various sizes, thirty thousand square feet of polished marble wainscoting, and over a mile of marble tiling eight feet wide. The equipment includes sixteen elevators, : eight pumps for operating the elevators and forcing water to large tanks on the roof, from which the house supply is taken, the total daily capacity being nine million gallons; four water-tube boilers of two hundred and fifty horse-power each; four tandem compound engines with attached dynamos of capacity to supply seven thousand incandescent electric lights; forty miles of distributing electric light wires, in iron armored conduits; six ventilating fans in hoods on the roof and one in the basement, capable of discharging twenty-one million cubic feet of air per hour. The wood-work throughout the building is natural oak.

The cost of the site and building complete was about three million three hundred and fifty thousand dollars. The style of architecture is the Italian renaissance.

Among the tenants of the Ellicott Square building are the Ellicott Square and Niagara Banks, on the second floor; the Western Union Telegraph Company, with one of the finest operating rooms in the world, and the Ellicott Club of six hundred representative business men, with beautiful and elaborately furnished rooms on the tenth floor.

MAIN STREET—LOOKING NORTH FROM NIAGARA STREET.

Erie County Savings Bank.

Not as large as Ellicott Square, but in a position equally as prominent, is the Erie County Savings Bank building, unlike any other structure in Buffalo, and undoubtedly among the handsomest in the United States. Fire-proof in the full sense, it is not of the steel frame manner of construction, nor does its support depend upon the strength of iron columns. Its walls hold it up—massive and yet beautiful walls, of a red-gray granite. that promise to endure for ages. Bounded by Niagara, Pearl and Church streets, and with an end facing Main street, the principal entrance is at Niagara. The facades are broken by round towers, with spire tops, and the steep roofs, covered with heavy red tiles, are terraced. The entire effect is picturesque in the extreme, and the magnificent building is justly an object of much local pride. Various marbles of exquisite coloring are profusely apparent in the finish of the banking rooms and corridors. Throughout the wood-work is of mahogany.

The site formerly was that of the old First Presbyterian Church, which stood there for some sixty years, and with its near Episcopal neighbor, St. Paul's, established "The Churches" as a landmark and guide, which did duty as such until the old First was razed. Its congregation joined the "up-town" movement, building a new brownstone church and chapel of the utmost elegance in the aristocratic neighborhood of North street and the Circle.

The bank building was completed in the spring of 1893. The cost was about one million one hundred thousand dollars, which was paid from the Erie County Savings Bank's surplus. This bank and the Fidelity Trust and

Guaranty Company occupy the first story. The seven
floors above are divided into offices.

On the west side of Main street, a short distance below
Erie, and bending so that another frontage on Erie street
is obtained, is the White building. Of red brick and iron,
and completed in 1881, it was the first fire-proof office
building erected in the city. Of seven stories, the ground
floor is one great store.

Passing other large and more or less impressive edifices
on the route down Main street, attention is arrested by
the beauty of the Bank of Buffalo's building, at the northwest corner of Seneca street. Occupied exclusively by
the bank, it is of white stone, with a large dome. On the
east side of Main street, below Seneca street, is the new
building of the Bank of Commerce, also of stone. It is
of purely classic architecture, but not situated for display
to best advantage. At the southwest corner of Main and
Seneca streets is the fine home of the Manufacturers and
Traders' Bank, formerly known as the Hayen building.
It is of iron and glass.

Board of Trade Building.

West Seneca street, between Main and Pearl streets, is
shadowed by tall bank buildings on the south side, and
the Board of Trade building on the north. When Central Wharf was abandoned as the market place for buying and selling grain, the business was moved to this
structure, which was completed in 1883. It was built by
the Board of Trade (organized in 1844), and is still owned
by that corporation; but the business is transacted by the
Merchants' Exchange, which was formed to widen the

THE STAR THEATRE.

sphere of operation so as to include the various branches of trade and commerce, in addition to the grain trade. Originally of seven stories and high basement, an eighth story has been added recently to the building.

Viewed from Main street, East Seneca street, one of the city's most important business thoroughfares, shows large, substantial blocks, as far as the eye can reach, notable among them being the Richmond building, and the commodious Broezel Hotel, at the corner of Wells street.

At the northeast corner of Seneca and Washington streets, is the Federal building, containing the general Post-office, and the Custom House, United States Court room, etc, Its material is freestone. This building has been long inadequate to the requirements. Agitation for a new home for the Government offices was years ago begun. The hopeful prospect now is that the edifice will be provided as soon as the work of its construction—now under way—can be done.

The New Post-office.

From numerous proposals, the government selected as a site for the projected Federal building—the New Post-office, as the people commonly say—the square bounded by Ellicott, South Division, Oak and Swan streets. This in the long ago was part of a fine residence district, that in later years went to decay. The selection gave an immediate boom to surrounding property, practically all of which was bought up at good prices by investors, and is held to await the business movement eastward, which they think the great Postoffice will be sure to attract.

Exactly east of Ellicott Square, and just one block dis-
tant, will be another great architectural pile, of even larger
ground dimensions. It will be twenty feet longer and
twenty feet wider than the Ellicott Square building. The
plans, at first prepared by the government, were adversely
criticised in many quarters, but have been revised in important features, and now promise a very handsome as
well as vast edifice. The foundations have been laid, and
stonework to the height of the water-table, the value of
the work done to the time of this writing being about
eighty thousand dollars. The stone is a rich red granite.

While the building, exclusive of the tower, will be of
but three stories, their height will be such that the total
height, including the part of the basement above ground,
and the pitched roof, will equal that of the ordinary nine-
story office building. Just when the new postoffice will be
finished, and just how big a sum will be its final cost, cannot at this day be foretold with any claim to accuracy;
but all Buffalo's people unite in the hope that there will be
no unnecessary delay.

Washington street, nearly its whole length, is given to
light manufacturing and mercantile business. It has many
substantial buildings devoted to these purposes. Corner-
ing at Exchange street is the large Washington block, in
which the *Morning Express* has its home. At the north
corner of Broadway, the Buffalo Savings Bank has a solidly
handsome structure of brown stone. A little further up
the street is the Lyceum Theater.

East of Washington street, at and above Chippewa
street, are the grounds and long building of one of the
city's four public markets. The others are on Elk street,
Clinton street and Broadway. North of the Washington

C. W. MILLER'S COACH, COUPE AND BAGGAGE
EXPRESS STABLES.

Market stands the stately St. Michael's church, of stone, and next is the three-story brick and stone structure of Canisius College, with frontage of over three hundred feet. This institution, directed by the Jesuit Fathers, was founded in 1870, and chartered by the Regents of the University of the State of New York in 1883.

The principal business streets of the east side are Elk street, which leads to South Buffalo; Seneca street, William street, Broadway and Genesee street.

Live Stock Exchange.

William street is the direct thoroughfare to the great Live Stock yards of East Buffalo, where it becomes a scene of much activity. The dealers have an ably managed Exchange, and in 1890 erected a commodious building for its occupancy. It is on William street, opposite the New York Central yards. Of brick, with stone trimmings, it is three stories in height.

On Broadway are several imposing church edifices, also the State Arsenal and Drill Hall of the Sixty-fifth Regiment, National Guard.

Returning now to Main street, and continuing the view south, the block between Seneca and Exchange streets is seen to contain the offices of three of the leading newspapers. At the south corner of Exchange street is the oldest of the city's prominent hotels, the Mansion House. Opposite its Main street front begins the broad sweep of the thoroughfare known as the Terrace, at the head of which stands the Liberty Pole, to which sentimental object Buffalo has persistently clung. The present pole is of iron, very tall and graceful. In the very old times a bluff

extended along the north line of the Terrace, the land
below, to Buffalo Creek, being marshy. West of Main
street and south of the Terrace is the city's most uninvit-
ing part.

Buffalo's Newspapers.

About seventy-five newspapers and trade, professional
and other periodicals, are published in Buffalo. There are
newspapers printed in German and in Polish.

The *Commercial* is the oldest of the dailies. Under the
name of the *Gazette*, it began as a weekly in the year 1810
or 1811. Its daily edition dates from 1835. Always ably
conducted, its political prestige was mainly secured under
the proprietorship of the late James D. Warren and the
late James N. Matthews. It has a solid standing with
the conservative element of the public. The *Commercial*
occupies its five-story fire-proof building at the southeast
corner of Washington and North Division streets.

On the east side of Main street, midway between Seneca
and Exchange streets, is the fine seven-story fire-proof
building from which the *Courier* is issued. This is one of
several structures comprised in the Courier Company's
great plant. The paper was established about the year
1831, but did not take its present name until 1845, when
it was published as the *Buffalo Courier* by Joseph String-
ham, who is still living at a very advanced age. The
paper has maintained a high reputation for the excellence
of its conduct and thought. No record of Buffalo, however summarized, would be satisfactory without at least
mention of such men as the late Joseph Warren and the
late David Gray, who editorially conducted this newspaper.

MUSIC HALL.

About it has been built up a vast lithographic, show and general printing business. The company's six-story edifice on Washington street was the first entirely fire-proof building built in Buffalo for any purpose.

The *Morning Express* was founded in 1846, by the veteran journalist and man of public affairs, Almon M. Clapp. After his retirement, the paper was not very prosperous until it went into the hands of James N. Matthews, who, removing it to his Washington Block, where it has since remained, practically re-created it as a newspaper.

On the west side of Main street, below Seneca, an elegant seven-story structural steel building is being erected for the *Evening News*. This paper was started as an independent weekly in 1873, by Adams & Butler. In a few years Mr. Adams retired. Edward H. Butler began the cheap daily edition in 1880, by his energetic management securing success for the enterprise.

The *Buffalo Times*, also in the cent newspaper field, was founded by Norman E. Mack as a weekly in 1877, and was made a daily in 1883. Its publication office is on Main street, next below the *Courier* office.

The youngest, but not the least active of the prominent newspapers, is the *Buffalo Enquirer*, now published by a company of which William J. Conners is the head. At this time a large building on the west side of Main street, between Swan and Seneca streets, is being prepared for its use.

Of the three daily papers printed in the German language, the *Demokrat*, the *Freie Presse* and the *Volksfreund*, the oldest is the *Demokrat*, established in 1837.

The Masonic Temple.

A good many years ago the Methodists built a stone church on the northeast side of Niagara street, near Franklin street. It is a commanding position, and the land now is nearly as valuable as any other in the city. The Methodists seldom record a failure, but they did in this case. They could not retain the property. The Christian church passed from their hands and became a Jewish synagogue. As such it continued until the wealthy congregation built a new temple elsewhere. Then it was razed and on its site stands the fine fire-proof building which serves as a home for most of the city's Masonic bodies.

The corner-stone of the Masonic Temple was laid in July, 1891, and the building was dedicated on the 20th of January, 1892. The facade indicates seven stories, but practically there are eight. The entire front is of brown stone, with a large arched entrance that is very handsome. The Acacia Club, exclusively composed of members of the Masonic fraternity, occupies the second floor. In the upper part of the edifice, two superb apartments, known as the Blue Room and the Scarlet Room, respectively accommodate the lodges, and the chapters and councils, etc. Also there are quarters for the commanderies of the Knights Templar, and a beautiful banquet hall. The cost of the Temple was one hundred and sixty-five thousand dollars.

City and County Hall.

When the city was very young, the land bounded by Franklin, Eagle, Delaware and Church streets, was the principal cemetery. The cholera epidemics soon filled it,

ST. LOUIS ROMAN CATHOLIC CHURCH.

and further sepulture in this ground was forbidden. Years afterwards, such bodies as had not become lost in the mother earth were removed to Forest Lawn, when Franklin Square became a public park, remaining as such until it was appropriated as the site for the structure which the city and county united to build to house their departments of government.

It is a common saying of Buffalo people that their City and County Hall is probably the best building in the world for the amount of money that it cost. It was built at a time when labor and materials were cheap ; and, perhaps more important, there was no jobbery in connection with the enterprise. Complete and furnished, within a million and a half was paid for the grand pile. The corner-stone was laid in 1872, and the building finished in 1876.

Of Norman architecture, the building is in the form of a double Roman cross, with central entrances facing Franklin street and Delaware avenue. The entire material of the walls and tower is granite, brought from Clark's Island, off the coast of Maine. The construction is grandly massive, with an imposing tower at the Franklin street front, reaching an altitude of two hundred and sixty-five feet. About the apex of the tower are four great granite statues, representing Justice, Commerce, Agriculture and Industry. Within, the corridors are paved and wainscoted with marble. All the interior woodwork is highly finished black walnut.

Built about the time that the City and County Hall was ready for use, the County Jail is on the opposite side of Delaware avenue. This castle-like structure of stone and iron cost two hundred thousand dollars.

When the City and County Hall was finished, it seemed
that it must be sufficient for at least a generation; but
when Buffalo took a fresh start, and began to grow as it
had never grown before, the public business grew with it.
The crowded condition of the hall became such that, for
its necessary relief, the Municipal Building, so called, was
in 1889 erected on Delaware avenue, just north of the jail.
This annex provides quarters for the Municipal Court, the
Department of Education, the Health Department, the
Bureau of Water and the Bureau of Building. As a further
relief, the addition of a fourth story to the City and County
Hall is now in contemplation.

St. Joseph's Cathedral.

Built of the limestone from Buffalo Plains, St. Joseph's
Roman Catholic Cathedral is on the west side of Franklin street at Swan street, and is a fine specimen of gothic
architecture. The corner-stone was laid in 1852. The
length of the edifice is two hundred and thirty-six feet.
Of its two towers, one is yet unfinished. The completed
tower contains one of the finest carillons in the world,
consisting of forty-three bells, made at Munich. Unfor-
tunately, the land where the cathedral rests is so low
lying, and the belfry is so inclosed, that the music of
these remarkable bells is seldom heard any considerable
distance; and, indeed, the very fact of their existence
probably is unknown to many residents of the city.
This cathedral also possesses the great Hook organ
which was exhibited at the Centennial Exposition at
Philadelphia.

THE 74TH REGIMENT ARMORY.

The Women's Union.

The Women's Educational and Industrial Union is a non-sectarian organization, whose sphere is generally indicated by its title. With more than a thousand members, it is one of the most powerful associations of women in America, and the amount of educational, protective and philanthropic work that it has done since its formation in 1884 can hardly be estimated. The Union has served as the model for similar societies in several other cities. It has an elegant building on Niagara Square—one of the old mansions of that locality reconstructed and materially enlarged.

The Fitch Institute.

The Charity Organization Society of Buffalo, for the regulation and intelligent distribution of charity, and the restriction of the evil of pauperism, was the first of its kind in this country. It was formed in 1877, and incorporated two years later. Its efficiency has been greatly aided by the ownership and operation of the Fitch Institute, a large brick building at the southwest corner of Swan and Michigan streets, erected from a munificent bequest received from the late Benjamin Fitch. It provides room for the excellently appointed Fitch Accident Hospital, and the Fitch Provident Dispensary, besides headquarters for the Fresh Air Mission, and other associations for the public welfare.

On Swan street, immediately north of the Fitch Institute, is the justly celebrated Fitch Creche, or Day Nursery, which also was the first in America, and has been the pattern for others.

Inclosed by Court, Franklin and West Genesee streets, is the Buffalo High School. For its overflow of several hundred pupils, an annex on Clinton street furnishes accommodations. A large and handsome new High School building on Masten Park, for the east side, is approaching completion. The city has in operation fifty-six Grammar schools, for which most of the buildings are of modern contruction.

Going north on Main street from Lafayette Square, the first large structure is the Tifft House. At Mohawk street one walks but a block to the handsome Star Theatre, facing Mohawk, Pearl and West Genesee streets; built especially for the purposes of the drama, its auditorium is charmingly attractive.

At West Genesee and Main streets is the Genesee, another of the city's hotels of the first class.

On the north side of Huron street, west of Franklin street, is Charles W. Miller's stable, in connection with his railroad transfer, coach and baggage business. The big six-story building is notable alike for its unusual size, and the perfection of system in its arrangement and management.

The Music Hall.

In 1883, the German Young Men's Association completed its Music Hall, designed for music festivals, conventions and other large gatherings; and as a home for the parent association, and several German musical societies. Two years later a tragical fire utterly destroyed the building, and the neighboring St. Louis Church as well. The

THE BUFFALO MEDICAL COLLEGE.

Music Hall arose from its ashes, larger and finer than
before. Of brick and iron, its frontage on Main street is
one hundred and eighty-eight feet, and on Edward street
two hundred and sixty-two feet. The main auditorium will
seat about two thousand five hundred persons. Within
the building is a smaller hall, with seating capacity for
about eleven hundred. It is the intention to soon trans-
form the principal hall, so that it will be better adapted for
dramatic entertainments.

The new St. Louis Roman Catholic Church, of brown
stone, at the north corner of Main and Edward streets, is
one of the handsomest and most costly in the city.

Buffalo Medical College.

The University of Buffalo, organized in 1845, has departments of medicine, dentistry, pharmacy, law and pedagogy.
The medical department is by far the oldest, and is of wide
repute. Its fine four-story building on High street, at
Main street, completed in 1893, is said to be among the
best in existence, as regards perfect adaptation to the uses
for which it was designed.

Niagara University also has a department of medicine,
with college building on Ellicott street.

On High street, east of the Buffalo Medical College
building, is the General Hospital, in which over two thousand patients were treated during the year 1895. One wing
of a magnificent new building, for this hospital, is in course
of construction. The estimated cost of the structure when
finished is about a quarter of a million.

The Armory.

On Virginia street, at Elmwood avenue, is the Armory built by the county for the Seventy-fourth Regiment, National Guard. It is a large structure—but not large enough, and lacking in other essentials. In pursuance of an agreement with the State, the City of Buffalo has deeded to the State the superb tract of land bounded by Niagara and Connecticut streets, Prospect avenue and Vermont street—formerly the site of a reservoir—on which the latter is pledged to build for the use of the regiment an armory to cost four hundred thousand dollars.

Sisters of Charity Hospital.

The Hospital of the Sisters of Charity was established in 1848, and in the nearly half a century of its existence has performed a work of incalculable good for suffering humanity. Its present buildings, including a wing but recently completed, are on outer Main street. About a quarter of a million has been expended in their erection. The institution maintains at the corner of South Division and Michigan streets an Emergency Hospital for the reception of accident cases.

Forest Lawn.

The two hundred and sixty and more acres of this most beautiful cemetery, inclosed by high iron fencing, are bounded by Main street, Delevan avenue, Delaware avenue and the North Park. There are entrances from Main street and Delaware. Scajaquada Creek runs directly

THE GENERAL HOSPITAL.

through the cemetery, here in a narrow rock bed, there broadened into lake-like expanse with delightful effects of woodland border. Bridges of arched stone carry the roadways across the creek. The grounds show a diversity of hill and valley, to which landscape art has added all possible charm.

Counted in the more than forty thousand graves, are those of many illustrious persons; and among the innumerable carved memorials are many monuments commanding in their magnificence. Those of a public character include the Red Jacket Monument and Statue, the Firemen's Monument, the Soldiers' Monument, in the Grand Army lot, and one erected by the city at the place of reinterment of the remains taken out of Franklin Square. Here are the graves of several officers and soldiers who were killed in the struggles for the possession of old Fort Erie.

Of other cemeteries in and about Buffalo, the most important are those at Pine Hill, and the large Roman Catholic Cemetery of the Holy Cross in the town of West Seneca.

State Hospital for the Insane.

Of public institutions in and near the city, other than those which have been enumerated, there is a large number, many of them with fine buildings which have been erected at great cost—the Erie County Penitentiary, the Limestone Hill Protectory, Buffalo Orphan Asylum, Episcopal Church Home, Buffalo Female Academy, State Normal School, Academy of the Holy Angels, St. Mary's Institute for Deaf Mutes, and a long list of others, each with

features of more than passing interest—but the limitations
of this book will not permit individual description of them
all; nor even a really adequate account of the greatest
among all charitable creations in Buffalo, the State Hospital for the Insane.

The magnitude of this splendid institution may be
inferred from the simple statement that the hospital proper,
a chain of buildings connected and made practically one
by curving fire-proof corridors, is more than half a mile
long. The tract of land, facing Forest avenue and lying a
little distance west of the North Park, was given by the city
as an inducement for the State to place the hospital here.
Twenty years ago it was remote from any thickly built-up
district, but now it overlooks one of the most delightful
residence parts. The corner-stone was laid in 1872, by
Governor John T. Hoffman. The chain of connected
buildings is as a bow, with the convex side toward Forest
avenue. This design secures much privacy, without that
essential feature seeming forced.

At the center is the administration building, a massive
structure of dark red stone, with two pointed towers. To
the east and the west of this stretch the ward buildings.
Four of these—two at each side—of three stories, are of
stone to correspond with the central edifice; four are of
brick, two stories high; and the two buildings which are
the ends of the bow, also of brick, are of but one story·
Each ward building has a central extension at the rear.
Originally the intention was to construct the entire hospital of stone, but the enormous cost led to a change of the
plans in this respect. To about the year 1890, only the
wards east of the administration building had been completed. Since then work has been pushed until the scheme

THE NEW HIGH SCHOOL.

is finished in its entirety, the assumption of the care of the pauper insane of the counties by the State having made urgent the need for the additional accommodations. On the grounds are numerous isolated structures, including kitchen, nurses' dormitory, engine house, laundry, stables, infirmary and a fine conservatory.

City of Homes.

Two hundred miles of the streets of Buffalo are paved with asphalt. Most of the streets covered with this material are lined by the homes of the people. By no means all of these are architecturally pretentious, but nearly every house has at least a bit of well-kept lawn, and the beauty of the streets with their clean white roadways, green turf between curb lines and sidewalks, and frequent rows of fine shade trees, is an incentive to householders to keep their premises in as attractive condition as their means will allow.

A street that long ago became famous is Delaware avenue. From Niagara Square to the Park approaches, it is lined with stately and often sumptuous residences, with broad grounds which have all the beauty to be derived from the gardener's art. Of buildings other than homes and churches, the most notable is the noble mansion of the Buffalo Club, at the north corner of Trinity street. At Edward street is the handsome house of the Saturn Club. Above Allen street is the beautiful new home of the Twentieth Century Club, an organization of women. Other club-houses in the city are those of the Phœnix Club, on Franklin street—just built—and the University Club, on Main street, north of Virginia street. Of the churches on

Delaware avenue, the most magnificent are the Delaware Avenue Methodist, Trinity Episcopal, the Delaware Avenue Baptist, and the beautiful and unique Jewish Temple Beth Zion.

But of the Buffalo of to-day Delaware avenue is only one of many superb residence streets. Perhaps the most aristocratic of all is the short stretch of North street from Delaware to the charming neighborhood of the Circle. Richmond avenue, Norwood avenue, Elmwood avenue, Summer street, West Ferry street—these and others are remarkable for the beauty of the homes which adorn them. North of North street and west of Delaware, far out to Forest avenue, the territory is paralleled and crossed by a multitude of streets that are of delightful attractiveness. Upper Franklin street, lovely Linwood avenue, and the exquisite Parkside district, are of other places where home-life ought to be a joy.

A city of elegant homes of the classes by fortune more favored, it is alike a city of homes of the working people. Probably in no other place in America do so many working men own the houses in which they live. About them flowers often bloom, while within, not infrequently, are evidences of comfort, refinement and content.

LAKE VIEW—FOREST LAWN.

BRIDGE VIEW—FOREST LAWN.

NEW YORK STATE HOSPITAL.

DELAWARE AVENUE SCENE.

GREATER BUFFALO.

The Electric City of the Future.

Since the achievement of the generation of electric energy by the power of Niagara Falls, and the demonstration of the feasibility of the transmission of the electrical current for considerable distances without appreciable waste, "the world is watching Buffalo" has become a familiar declaration. The grand experiments at Niagara Falls enlisted the interest of scientests all over the earth. At the outset, there was a marked division of opinion as to the probable success or failure. When success became apparent, another division, with much discussion, ensued, over the transmission question. One of the leading American electrical journals editorially and unequivocally asserted that to transmit the power from the place of production to Buffalo without such loss as to make the undertaking commercially disastrous, was impossible. But upon this point no doubt now seems to remain. Even savants sometimes may be mistaken. And, then, this matter of the generation and application of electricity is all so new! Fifty years ago the galvanic battery was a curious plaything. Twenty years ago the telephone was not in public use.

The stage of experiment successfully passed, the industrial world is eagerly looking for results. Where power may be had the cheapest, there naturally must manufactories thrive, and new ones be attracted to the so favored field, if shipping facilities and other imperatively required conditions are right. Buffalo reasonably is expected to reap the greatest benefit from the new motive force. Contracts have been closed for the construction of a transmission line, a company has been formed for the distribution of the power within the city, and the first installment of one thousand horse-power, which will be used by the Buffalo Railway Company, is guaranteed to be here in November of this year. The line will be equipped to transmit ten thousand horse-power, which may be increased to forty thousand by the stringing of additional wires—to receive which the poles are prepared—the latter amount being estimated as four-fifths of all the power used in the city of Buffalo at the present time. The power brought to the city's door and offered for sale, its relative price undoubtedly will fix the measure of the demand.

The direct power of Niagara Falls long has been used for the operation of mills in the immediate vicinity. Many years ago a hydraulic canal was dug to aid this purpose, taking its water from above the cataract, and discharging it over the bank below. Since 1892, this canal has been enlarged by the Niagara Falls Hydraulic Power Company, and apparatus provided for the generation of electric power in large quantity.

Far more formidable was the undertaking embraced in the scheme of the Niagara Falls Power Company. Skeptics there were in plenty to scoff at it, and predict that the millions proposed to be expended would be thrown away; but some of the heaviest and brainiest capitalists of the country—men who seldom put money where it will not earn more—had faith in the enterprise, had confidence in the experts employed to advise them, and furnished the means for a plant for the production of electricity in

ENCE OF CHARLES H. WILLIAMS.

amount practically without limit. To provide this plant
the Cataract Construction Company was organized. A
tunnel, seven thousand feet long, nineteen feet wide and
twenty-one feet high, has been completed. Water enters
it from above the Falls, and is emptied below, at the river's
edge. With such an incline, the force of the water rush-
ing through the tunnel must be prodigious, almost beyond
comprehension. Into the line of the tunnel, wheel-pits are
sunk, in which gigantic turbines are placed, these in turn
operating monster dynamos in the power-house. As
many of these turbines and dynamos can be used as the
demand for electric power may require.

With the very low-priced power which seems assured,
coupled with unsurpassed advantages of location, it is
justly believed that this city, enlarged, must become one of
the world's greatest manufacturing points, as it is already
one of the greatest commercial centers. There is said to
be force in the flowing water of Niagara River to generate
enough electricity to move all the machinery of the earth.
When the present plants are worked to their full capacity,
others can be provided. The construction of another tunnel at the Falls, on the Canada side, is contemplated.
Indeed, it seems that nothing but the demand need limit
the supply; and it may almost be added that nothing but
the price need limit the demand. In the words of a sanguine and imaginative believer in the grand results to
accrue to this locality from electricity, "We are coming
into the white light of the world's greatest progress. We,
in Buffalo, Niagara Falls, the Tonawandas, La Salle, all
along the Niagara Frontier, are entering the great theatre
of electrical development. We will head the procession
that is to enter the temple of wonders."

But while immense benefit to Buffalo from the electric power is certain, her magnificent destiny is not dependent or conditional upon this power, or any other artificial influence. Who can say, in fact, that in the future electricity may not be generated by much simpler and inexpensive means—gathered out of the air, as it were—so needing no Niagara Falls and costly tunnels. However improbable this seems, who now dares say that it is impossible? Whatever happens in this regard, though, Buffalo must profit from electricity, at least equally with any other place. And nature appears to have ordained that one great city shall extend the length of the Niagara Frontier. The forces that must lead to that result are in operation.

Each year enough people for a city of goodly size are added to Buffalo's population. Each year the ratio of the increase enlarges. As has been noted, it is a very long time since an extension of the limits was made. At present, however, annexation is a topic of active interest, and, no doubt, the legislature of the coming winter will be asked to authorize the acquisition of considerable territory, including the south village of Tonawanda. The populous suburbs call for improvements and protection which they can acquire only as parts of the city, under the city charter. To the east and southeast, Buffalo has grown well over the line into the towns of Cheektowaga and West Seneca. A few miles from the city's border, on the New York Central Railroad, is the bustling and thrifty new industrial village of Depew. Buffalo in time is sure to grow out to Depew, and Depew as certainly will reach on to the village of Lancaster.

At the north, the city line is but a little distance from the Tonawanda line. The two Tonawandas, the south

THE BUFFALO CLUB.

village in Erie County and the north one in Niagara County, are separated only by a bridged creek. Beyond North Tonawanda are the suburbs of Gratwick and Ironton; then La Salle, and less than three miles further, the city of Niagara Falls. It has been estimated that less than three hundred thousand people are needed to fill all these places, and the intervening spaces for a width of two miles, to Buffalo's present density. True, the city of to-day has room for many more inhabitants; some of its districts, no doubt, will be much more thickly populated; but the tendency toward parts where land is cheap and air is pure, is stimulated by the steadily improving means for rapid transit. Even if the recent ratio of increase of population became stationary, only about a dozen years would suffice to bring the numerical growth required by the estimate which has been quoted, for the continuous city from Lake Erie to and beyond the great cataract, if the entire tendency of settlement should be toward the north. The reasonable presumption is that it will be chiefly along the power transmission line, where multitudiuous new industries in all likelihood will be planted. Settlements will grow until they merge; the thousand and one agencies for providing necessaries and comforts must operate; and so business and population must increase, in an arithmetical progression.

Grand Island, too, as well as the entire mainland frontage of the upper Niagara, will be taken into the Greater Buffalo—no enthusiast's dream or romance of the land boomer, but the certain, logical consequence of the filling up and continued enrichment of the almost boundless region made by nature tributary to it.

RESIDENCE OF GEORGE V. FORMAN.

TEMPLE BETH ZION.

RESIDENCE OF WILLIAM HAMLIN.

VIEW ON NORTH STREET.

RESIDENCE OF EDMUND HAYES.

THE FIRST PRESBYTERIAN CHURCH.

VIEW ON SUMMER STREET.

RESIDENCE OF P. H. GRIFFIN.

PROGRAMME

OF THE

TENTH CONVENTION

OF THE

NATIONAL ASSOCIATION OF BUILDERS

TUESDAY, SEPTEMBER 15th, 1896.

Morning Session.

Address of Welcome by Mayor of the City of Buffalo.

Address by President of the Buffalo Exchange.

Address by President of the National Association of Builders.

Appointment of Committee on Credentials.

Afternoon Session.

Report of Committee on Credentials,

Roll Call.

Appointment of Committee on time and place of next Convention, and nomination of Officers.

Annual Report of Secretary.

Annual Report of Treasurer.

Consideration of the following requests presented by the Master Builders' Association of Boston :

> 1st. That the National Association of Builders take action in support of the movement to create an expert commission to have charge of all architectural work of the United States Government.

2d. That the National Association of Builders recommend all filial bodies to secure an amendment to the building laws of their various cities looking toward the creation of Boards of Appeal.

3d. That the National Association of Builders recommend the Joint Committee on Uniform Contract to secure an amendment to the Uniform Contract, so that payments shall be called for under the contract IN GOLD rather than in "current funds," as the said contract now reads.

Presentation and Reference of Resolutions.

WEDNESDAY, SEPTEMBER 16th.
Morning Session.

Consideration of Amendments to Constitution.

Consideration of the question—

"Are organizations of builders, either local or national, desirable? If so, what are the functions of such bodies? And should the value of organization be measured by or dependent upon immediate specific results only?"

THURSDAY, SEPTEMBER 17th.

There will be no session of the Convention on Thursday.

FRIDAY, SEPTEMBER 18th.
Morning Session.

Report of Committees on Resolutions.

Report of Committee on time and place for next Convention and nomination of Officers.

Election of Officers.

Unfinished Business.

Miscellaneous.

OFFICERS AND DIRECTORS

OF THE

NATIONAL ASSOCIATION OF BUILDERS

FOR THE YEAR 1896.

President,
CHARLES A. RUPP, Buffalo.

First Vice-President,
H. J. SULLIVAN, Milwaukee.

Secretary,
WILLIAM H. SAYWARD, Boston.

Treasurer,
GEORGE TAPPER, Chicago.

Directors,

Baltimore, .	NOBLE H. CREAGER.
Boston, .	E. NOYES WHITCOMB.
Buffalo, .	. JOHN FEIST.
Chicago,	. WILLIAM GRACE.
Detroit, .	RICHARD HELSON.
Lowell, .	. FRANK L. WEAVER.
Milwaukee,	. . LOUIS A. CLAS.
New York,	STEPHEN M. WRIGHT.
Philadelphia,	. STACY REEVES.
Providence,	. . THOMAS B. ROSS.
Rochester,	JUSTUS HERBERT GRANT.
St. Louis, .	. THOMAS J. WARD.
St. Paul, .	GEORGE J. GRANT.
Wilmington,	. . . A. S. REED.
Worcester,	GEORGE H. CUTTING.

... ROSTER ...

OF THE

NATIONAL ASSOCIATION OF BUILDERS

First Convention at Chicago, 1887.

President—GEORGE C. PRUSSING, Chicago.
Vice-President—J. MILTON BLAIR, Cincinnati.
Secretary and Treasurer—WILLIAM H. SAYWARD, Boston.

Second Convention at Cincinnati, 1888.

President—J. MILTON BLAIR, Cincinnati.
1st Vice-President—JOHN S. STEVENS, Philadelphia.
2d Vice-President—EDWARD E. SCRIBNER, St. Paul.
Secretary—WILLIAM H. SAYWARD, Boston.
Treasurer—JOHN J. TUCKER, New York, N. Y.

Third Convention at Philadelphia, 1889.

President—JOHN S. STEVENS, Philadelphia.
1st Vice-President—EDWARD E. SCRIBNER, St. Paul.
2d Vice-President—JOHN J. TUCKER, New York, N. Y.
Secretary—WILLIAM H. SAYWARD, Boston.
Treasurer—GEORGE TAPPER, Chicago.

Fourth Convention at St. Paul, 1890.

President—EDWARD E. SCRIBNER, St. Paul.
1st Vice-President—JOHN J. TUCKER, New York, N. Y.
2d Vice-President—ARTHUR McALLISTER, Cleveland.
Secretary—WILLIAM H. SAYWARD, Boston.
Treasurer—GEORGE TAPPER, Chicago.

Fifth Convention at New York, 1891.

President—JOHN J. TUCKER, New York, N. Y.
1st Vice-President—ARTHUR McALLISTER, Cleveland.
2d Vice-President—ANTHONY ITTNER, St. Louis.
Secretary—WILLIAM H. SAYWARD, Boston.
Treasurer—GEORGE TAPPER, Chicago.

Sixth Convention at Cleveland, 1892.

President—ARTHUR McALLISTER, Cleveland.
1st Vice-President—ANTHONY ITTNER, St. Louis.
2d Vice-President—IRA G. HERSEY, Boston.
Secretary—WILLIAM H. SAYWARD, Boston.
Treasurer—GEORGE TAPPER, Chicago.

Seventh Convention at St. Louis, 1893.

President—ANTHONY ITTNER, St. Louis.
1st Vice-President—IRA G. HERSEY, Boston.
2d Vice-President—HUGH SISSON, Baltimore.
Secretary—WILLIAM H. SAYWARD, Boston.
Treasurer—GEORGE TAPPER, Chicago.

Eighth Convention at Boston, 1894.

President—IRA G. HERSEY, Boston.
1st Vice-President—NOBLE H. CREAGER, Baltimore.
2d Vice-President—CHARLES A. RUPP, Buffalo.
Secretary—WILLIAM H. SAYWARD, Boston.
Treasurer—GEORGE TAPPER, Chicago.

Ninth Convention at Baltimore, 1895.

President—NOBLE H. CREAGER, Baltimore.
1st Vice-President—CHARLES A. RUPP, Buffalo.
2d Vice-President—JAMES MEATHE, Detroit.
Secretary—WILLIAM H. SAYWARD, Boston.
Treasurer—GEORGE TAPPER, Chicago.

List of Exchanges Entitled to Representation at the Tenth Convention.

Baltimore, Md.

The Builders Exchange, Lexington and Charles Streets.

Boston, Mass.

The Master Builders Association, 166 Devonshire Street.

Buffalo, N. Y.

The Builders Association Exchange, Court and Pearl Sts.

Chicago, Ill.

The Builders and Traders Exchange, 34 Clark Street.

Detroit, Mich.

The Builders and Traders Exchange, 92 Fort Street.

Lowell, Mass.

The Builders Exchange, 14 Appleton Street.

Milwaukee, Wis.

The Builders and Traders Exchange, Grand Avenue and Fifth Street.

New York, N. Y.

The Mechanics and Traders Exchange, 117 East Twenty-third Street.

Philadelphia, Pa.

The Master Builders Exchange, 18-24 South Seventh St.

Providence, R. I.

The Builders and Traders Exchange, 44 and 48 Custom House Street.

Rochester, N. Y.

Builders and Building Supply Dealers Exchange, 27 E. Main Street.

St. Louis, Mo.

The Builders Exchange, Bell Telephone Building, Tenth and Olive Streets.

St. Paul, Minn.

The Builders Exchange, Seventh and Cedar Streets.

Wilmington, Del.

The Builders Exchange, 605 Market Street.

Worcester, Mass.

The Builders Exchange, Knowles Building.